From th_ ....

Mary M. Cushnie-Mansour

**A collection of short stories with snippets of life,
introducing you to characters that
will take you inside their hearts and souls
to help you learn a little something about yourself...**
Richard Beales (former editor/Brantford Expositor)

From the Heart

Author's/Publisher's Note: This is a work of fiction. Names, characters, places, and incidents are a product of the author's imagination unless otherwise noted. Locales and public names are sometimes used for atmospheric purposes. Any resemblance to actual people, living or dead, or to businesses, companies, events, institutions, or locales are entirely coincidental unless otherwise noted.

From the Heart can be ordered through Amazon or the author's website: http://www.writerontherun.ca

Cover Art - Natasja Hellenthal
http://www.beyondbookcovers.com

Cover Layout - Terry Davis
http://www.ballmedia.com

Printed by
Brant Service Press
Brantford, ON

ISBN 978-1-989027-17-2
2nd Edition

CAVERN
OF DREAMS
PUBLISHING
http://www.cavernofdreamspublishing.com

Books by Mary M. Cushnie-Mansour

Night's Vampire Series
Night's Gift
Night's Children
Night's Return
Night's Temptress
Night's Betrayals
Night's Revelations

Detective Toby Series
Are You Listening to Me
Running Away From Loneliness
Past Ghosts

Short Stories
From the Heart
Mysteries From the Keys

Poetry
picking up the pieces
Life's Roller Coaster
Devastations of Mankind
Shattered
Memories

Biographies
A 20th Century Portia

Youth Novels
A Story of Day & Night   The Silver Tree

Bilingual Picture Books
The Day Bo Found His Bark/Le jour où Bo trouva sa voix
Charlie Seal Meets a Fairy Seal/Charlie le phoque rencontre une fée
Charlie and the Elves/Charlie et les lutins
Jesse's Secret/Le Secret de Jesse
Teensy Weensy Spider/L'araignée Riquiqui
The Temper Tantrum/La crise de colère
Alexandra's Christmas Surprise/La surprise de Noël d'Alexandra
Curtis The Crock/Curtis le crocodile
Freddy Frog's Frolic/La gambade de Freddy la grenouille

Picture Books
The Official Tickler
The Seahorse and the Little Girl With Big Blue Eyes
Curtis the Crock
The Old Woman of the Mountain
Dragon Disarray

Author's Note

Many of these stories appeared in my newspaper column in the Brantford Expositor from 2006 to 2009. I would like to thank David Judd, who was the managing editor at the time, for opening the door for me into the world of freelancing and column writing. It was also a pleasure to work with Richard Beales, my column editor.

I was overwhelmed with the reception my stories received from the readers in Brantford, and appreciated all the magnificent comments that were sent my way. After my column was cancelled, I published the first version of "*From the Heart*," and it has been so successful, I have decided to publish a second edition. Many of the original stories are there, plus some new ones. Of course, the book has travelled far beyond the borders of my home town now!

I would like to thank everyone who inspired my stories by telling me snippets of their life, which I took and created a new tale based upon some truth and some fiction. Other stories are gleaned from my observations of life around me.

"*From the Heart*" are narratives from my heart to yours. Some will make you laugh; some will make you cry; some will make you wonder about the mystery of life. I hope you will enjoy reading them as much as I enjoyed writing them.

Mary M. Cushnie-Mansour,
Your Writer on the Run

http://www.writerontherun.ca

mary@writerontherun.ca

*Dedicated to
my family and friends
for their
continuous support of
my dream*

Table of Contents

The Fingers

I waited a long time for this moment in my life and now that I have finally arrived, my fingers tell me it will be short-lived!

Sixty words a minute, I used to type on an electronic typewriter. One hundred and twenty words a minute, I used to scribe across the pages with a fine point pen as I would listen and take notes in shorthand. But now, my fingers tell me to put these memories behind me and get ready for reality.

I inherited these fingers from my mother; she inherited hers from her father; from which side of the family he got his, I am not sure. They are nasty fingers that have followed my family tree down through the generations, picking randomly which one of us shall be the next victim.

When my mother gave birth to me in 1953, I had ten beautiful fingers. I have now lived more than half a century, as have those ten delicate fingers. But, something is different about them now: they are not all the same, and I fear that once some of them usurp the clan, the others will soon follow. They will shadow the leader.

First, arthritis set into my baby finger. The bones bubble oddly and painfully. The ring finger, next to the baby, was sympathetic; at times, it embraced some of the pain like a mother would do for her child. I feared the worst for them both, and for the tremendous tall father finger, and the baby's brothers and sisters. Which one of them would fall victim next? I soon learned all their fates!

My heart bleeds for these fingers, but also for the passion they will no longer be able to assist me with once the bubbles become too large and inflamed. Whatever will I do? Who will pound out the great novels I have dreamed of writing all my life? Who will be able to keep up with my creative mind as I spill the words from my soul? Who will understand my madness enough to translate it to the blank pages? That has been the job of my fingers, and now...

I have waited impatiently for these moments—my moments of the realization of my dream—and now I may be cheated of that dream because of the family tree of faulty body parts. Why could not this disease have started in my baby toe? It is not needed to write a novel, or a poem, or a song—only for the dance I never seem to get to perform!

Enough procrastination—I must hurry. Time runs out for my fingers. I have so much to impart to you, to release before the bubbles break my rhythm. So be ready, my friend, for my floodgate of madness is about to be spilled upon the soil: drink from it while you still can, for soon my fingers shall be gone!

Dear Patch

Winter in North Hampton hadn't changed much over the 90 years Winifred had lived there: it was still cold and damp, tormented by dreary, drizzling rain that seemed to go on forever. Winifred wandered around her tiny, ground-level flat. It had been twelve years since her husband Joseph had left, and her children didn't seem to have much time for her anymore.

Winifred sat down at her kitchen table and ran her fingers up and down the old cribbage board. She loved playing crib, but there wasn't anyone around to give her a good game. Well, Patch, her oldest son could, but he lived in Canada, and only came around once a year for two or three weeks. But when he did, they sure had some good games!

Winifred glanced at the calendar. It seemed like forever since he'd been over for a visit, yet it had only been three months. "Time sure flies when yer an old bird," she mumbled, "but, come to think of it, Patch, I ain't heard from yu fer a while." She pushed the cribbage board aside and reached for the phone. She kept most everything, of any importance, on the table so she could remember where it was.

She flipped through her phone book, looking for Patch's number. "Well, son, ifn' yu won't call me, I'll call you!" She dialled, let it ring ten times, and then slammed the receiver down. "He's never home—out havin' fun probably while I'm over here wastin' away, full 'o pain, sufferin' to no end…"

Over the next couple days, Winifred tried several times to reach Patch. She knew her family here in England was busy and they'd get around to her eventually, but it was Patch she was missing—especially their crib games! Finally, frustrated with her lack of success, Winifred decided to send him a letter. "Yu may not be answerin' yer phone, but I'm sure yu'll open yer mail, and I knows yu kin read cause I sent yu to school, and I have a lot to say to yu…" Winifred began to write:

Dear Patch:

After trying to unsuccessfully reach you by phone, I have decided the old way of writing, hoping to get thru to you, just to find out how thins are with you, how's that knee of yers progressing, I do hope having it seen to has made a good difference to it. I am in pain with my right foot, my toes burn like hell, keep me awake thru the nite, painkillers aren't touching it, it's just about driving me nuts, another thing to put up with in my (Golden Years) Joke!! I feel down in the dumps these days, and not hearing from you, is making me feel worse—I look forward to hearing your voice at times, also miss seeing you, no-one gives me a good game of crib like you do, I play a game of Scrabble with Linda, but it's only <u>once</u> <u>a</u> <u>month</u>, and no-one plays cribbage <u>at</u> <u>all</u>. I feel isolated and cut off from the world these days, I tried to get Tony's son Mark to have a game of scrabble with me, we played one game (I won) but he is very busy now he has got a new job—most of his work he has to do at home or travelling to different places, so that cuts me out. I very rarely see Steve; he's too busy playing at cops and robbers, and doing his regular job, only gets in touch with me when Linda tics him off for not seeing me. I feel isolated from family life these days, its "Bloody Lonely;" if I were younger you wouldn't see my ass for dust, I would have been over to see you, but life plays a dirty trick on me these days, I ain't the woman I used to be, mores the pity. If you can, Patch, please ring me—let it ring a long time

'cause I am <u>slow</u> getting to the phone from my chair. Also, my hearing is poor these days—<u>Poor ole sod, eh!</u>
Love ya Patch xxxx
  Mom xxxxxx

    On the back of the envelope, Winifred stuck a best wishes sticker. By the pink flower, she wrote, *To Patch, from mum xxxxxxx.* Beside it was another sticker, with her address and a picture of a kitten. Under that, she wrote the word *"sender."*

    Winifred decided to call the Complex Warden to post the letter. "I don't ask much of 'im," she declared, "bout time I started gettin' somethin' fer me pense!"

***

    Patch opened the letter from England. As he read it, tears ran down his leathery cheeks. He picked up the phone...

    "Mom?"

    "Patch!—you ol' sod—it's about time you give yer ol' mom a call!"

    Patch cleared his throat, "How you doin' mom?"

    "Didn't you read my letter?" she yelled, and then they both started to laugh.

Donald's Day

Donald rested against the cherry tree. It had been a long morning—he'd managed to pick six eleven quart baskets—he needed twelve. He popped a couple cherries in his mouth. Juicy red liquid dribbled down his chin. He looked up at the sky; it was almost noon.

"Guess I'll stop and eat now," he said while walking over to the tree where he'd left his lunch. His mom had packed his favourite sandwich, cheese on fresh home-made bread. He'd almost eaten it before he'd started picking the cherries, but had thought twice because he knew he'd be hungry at noon if he did. Also, there was the fact that if he went up to the house before he was finished the twelve baskets, he'd catch the end of the broom from his mom!

Donald bit into his sandwich. Mom made the best bread! He remembered back to when the family had lived in Hamilton and how he used to help his mom. She'd pull a chair up to the counter and let him measure the flour into her big wooden mixing bowl. Sometimes she'd even let him knead the dough.

When the bread came out of the oven, and after it cooled, he'd help her wrap the loaves in wax paper so his dad could make his daily deliveries. Donald never went on those; only his older brothers did.

After the sandwich was finished, Donald took a few gulps of water. It was warm, even though he'd wrapped a thick towel around the bottle to try and keep it cool.

"Sure is a hot one," he mumbled, wiping his brow. He glanced up to the sky. Clear as a bell overhead but there was some greying in the distance. Donald hoped it would cloud over and rain; then he wouldn't have to pick cherries for another three or four hours—especially if there were thunder and lightning!

Donald decided to close his eyes for a few minutes. His dad wouldn't be by to pick up the baskets of cherries for a while. He'd read in a book how some countries took a siesta at this time of day, and he envied those people. A dream crowded in on Donald's siesta...

He was by an ocean shore, lying in a hammock. There was a table laden with food within arm's reach—loaves of freshly baked bread, blocks of cheese, and baskets of ripe cherries. A huge pitcher of chocolate milk sat at one end.

Donald sat up and began to eat his fill. The cheese melted into the still-hot bread. He wiped his chin with the back of his hand when some cheese oozed out of the sandwich and then he popped some cherries into his mouth. He washed the meal down with the entire jug of milk.

"Ah, this is the life," he said and lay back in the hammock, placing his arms behind his head. The hammock began swinging gently as a light breeze blew through the palm trees. Clouds began to cover the sun. The breeze intensified, and the tree branches began dancing vigorously.

A drop of water landed on Donald's nose. He bolted up! Where was the table of food? Where was his hammock? His dream was over, but his wish was definitely coming true!

While sleeping, dark thunder clouds had rolled in. Donald glanced down the row of trees and saw a sheet of rain coming toward him. A humungous black cloud hovered overhead and a flash of lightning, followed by a thundering roar, echoed throughout the orchard.

Donald decided there was only one thing to do— head for home. He turned and began to run. He could hear the rain right behind him. It was getting close. The wind picked up. The cloud above danced furiously. More lightning. More thunder. A tree, somewhere to the left, cracked and then fell to the ground.

Donald found an extra spurt of adrenaline as raindrops pummelled the ground just behind him. One of his old runners flew off, but Donald pushed forward. The house came into view—there was still sunshine there. That gave him hope!

Finally … almost there … Donald's face was redder than his hair; his freckles bulged all over his arms … he was almost out of the woods … up the stairs … hand on the doorknob … black cloud scowling … rain vibrating on the roof … doorknob not turning…

"Mom! Let me in!" he yelled as he pounded on the door. Then he saw the note:

Donald, if you get back early from your cherry picking, the key is under the clothespin basket, by the back door. I have gone into Vineland with your dad. Love Mom.

Donald leaned against the door and sank down to the step. He began to laugh as the rain poured over his sweaty body!

Gilbert

*Dedicated to those
who have lost a loved one through cancer*

It was a long trek for Gilbert, but he couldn't miss this event. He smiled when he saw Becky standing guard at the back gate, making sure no one snuck in without paying, but she'd let him in—she always did.

"Why Gilbert, you old son of a gun!" Becky laughed. "Its bin too long; where ya bin hidin'?"

"Don't git aroun' much anymore," Gilbert smiled. "Got real bad arthritis in my joints."

Becky gave Gilbert an enormous hug. "Git in here … need a drink?"

"Water will do fer now."

Becky fetched him some water. "I got a few things to look after, so I'll catch ya later. Some of the old gang should be along shortly."

Gilbert was thankful they hadn't arrived yet. He felt weird this year, couldn't figure why. He found an empty picnic table and sat down. The crowd began to trickle in. A band was tuning up for their first session.

Becky studied her old friend. He had aged. His hair and beard were snow white, except for a red strip down the middle of his beard. Some might mistake it for red hair—she knew better—Gilbert chewed tobacco. She smiled as she noticed the length of his braid. Thirty years ago he swore he'd never cut it off. Becky wondered if he was bald under the bandana that he always wore. He was wearing glasses this year—a funny little round pair—made him look like a possum. Becky noticed the torn black jeans, greasy work boots, and the picture of a wolf on his shirt. *Wolf Man* was his nickname, back in the day.

Becky shuddered. She had a strange feeling something terrible was about to happen.

Gilbert lit a cigarette. Smoke curled around his head. He felt the tightness in his chest and began coughing. "Damn cigarettes," he cursed as he coughed up a massive gob of sputum. He gazed around, making sure no one was looking, and then spit under the table.

The band was playing some 50's rock and roll. They were old boys, like him. He glanced over to the entrance and noticed his buddy Roy heading toward him. "Hey, old man!" Roy shouted.

"I ain't hard of hearing; don't have to yell," Gilbert laughed. "How ya doin'?"

"Deaf," Roy was still shouting. "And can't afford hearin' aids."

"Gettin' old sucks, doesn't it?" Gilbert stated. "I'll be 70 next month, if'n I makes it."

"You don't say," Roy lit a cigarette.

Gilbert got a faraway look in his eyes. "Had a decent life, done what I wanted, when I wanted … faithful friends, good times…"

The two friends began to reminisce about their biker days. Finally, the announcement Gilbert had been waiting for came over the loudspeakers. "Anyone with pledges for getting their head shaved for cancer, please register up here. Our barbers will begin at 4:00 sharp."

"That's my cue." Gilbert got up from the table, shuffled to the registration table, dug into his pocket, pulled out his last month's disability cheque, and handed it to the girl. "Don't have a pledge sheet Miss, kin ya make me up one?"

"I'm not sure if we can take this cheque sir; I'll have to verify it with Becky."

"It's okay, Becky knows all about this." Gilbert didn't want to draw unnecessary attention to what he was about to do.

The girl filled out Gilbert's registration and put the cheque into a box. "Have a seat over there, Gilbert. Next, please."

Becky could not believe what she saw on the stage. Her old friend was taking off his bandana. Bald as a bald eagle he was. Everyone was gathering around to watch the main event. One of the musicians grabbed the microphone. "First up is Gilbert. Look at this ponytail folks—all the way to his waist—how many years did it take you to grow that Gilbert?"

"Too many," Gilbert whispered huskily.

"Well, folks, anyone want to sweeten the pot a little before Gilbert gets shaved?"

People began throwing coins and bills into Gilbert's box. He smiled as he recognized several old bikers dropping in some large bills. It would be a good day. The young hairdresser revved up her barber sheers. One cut and she waved the ponytail in the air. The crowd cheered! More money was dropped in the box!

No one noticed the tears trickle from Gilbert's eyes. No one noticed Becky wipe her face with an old hanky she had pulled out of her apron pocket. No one saw the embroidery in its corner: *"To Becky, my true love, from your Wolf Man – 1956."*

Gilbert slipped quietly away before Becky could reach him. She had a feeling she'd never see him again. Later that night, as she counted the proceeds, she came across his cheque. The tally for the money in Gilbert's box was $1, 657. 25. She turned his cheque over…

"Well, Becky, my love, this is it … the old Harley awaits me … I'll keep the back seat warm for you … take as long as you like. Love, your Wolf Man."

Becky's tears flowed shamelessly onto the words, smearing the message into an illegible swirl of ink.

Grandma "D"

Dorothy Marshall was her name, but everyone called her Grandma "D." Jason had lived with her since he was ten—she was old then. He'd been told if he messed up there, it was the end of the line for him.

Grandma "D" didn't say much and didn't have a lot of rules, but one thing she insisted on was respect. "You won't get anywhere in life, Jason, without respect for others, and yourself," she'd said.

Jason was playing Junior "A" hockey now, and his biggest fan was Grandma "D." She never missed a game. He recalled the day she'd signed him up. He'd been playing hockey at the neighbourhood rink, and she'd been watching from her living room window. At supper, there'd been an envelope beside his plate.

"What's this for?" he'd asked.

Grandma "D" had smiled. "I thought you might like to play hockey on a real team this winter."

"But the teams are already selected," Jason said.

"Father McNab has an opening on his team—one of the boys moved away."

Jason hadn't been sure about playing church hockey, but to play for a real team, well that was beyond his wildest dreams. He opened the envelope and saw two crisp one hundred dollar bills.

"If you don't want to play hockey," Grandma "D" began, "use the money for something else."

Jason's eyes had widened, "Anything I want?"

"Yep, as long as it's respectful. The team has a game in the morning at 7:00. If you want to play, Father McNab said to just show up."

Jason had hidden his joy as he shoved the envelope in his pocket and headed to his room. As Grandma "D" had watched him go, she whispered a silent prayer.

The next morning she was up early. The clock clicked to 6:45—still no Jason. Suddenly, he came bounding down the stairs.

"I'm not too late, am I?" he shouted.

She smiled. "No, we can make it!"

That was ten years ago. Tonight, Jason was being honoured with the "Most Valuable Player" award, and next season he'd be playing in the NHL. The ceremony began. Jason noticed Grandma "D" in her usual spot. She was wrapped in a blanket. She'd mentioned her arthritis was starting to best her.

Coach Benson was at the microphone. "I have the honour tonight to hand out the Most Valuable Player award to a young man who will be moving on to bigger things next season. We'll miss you, number 22. Jason Marshall, come forward, please."

As Jason received the trophy, his teammates pounded the ice with their sticks. "Speech … speech…" they chanted.

Jason smiled and set his trophy on the ice. He stepped up to the microphone and pulled an envelope from his pocket.

"Tonight is a special night indeed," he began, "ten years ago I was privileged to meet an extraordinary lady who took me into her home and treated me as her son. She gave me the opportunity to play hockey and somehow always found the money to ensure I could continue. At the Junior "A" level, while others had to look for personal sponsors, she dug into her wallet and came up with the funds.

"Over the years I've listened to the snickers from other teams when they read "Grandma D" on my shirt, but I just smile, knowing they really don't understand.

"It didn't stop at the monetary giving; Grandma "D" has not missed one of my games. Even now, afflicted with arthritis, she is here, bundled beneath her blanket. She is my biggest fan—my supreme mentor!

"Tonight, I pay tribute to her, for it is she who truly deserves to be honoured." Jason motioned to his team-mates, and they began skating toward Grandma "D." They gathered around, lifted her up, and skated over to Jason.

Father McNab came in, carrying a picture of Jason in full uniform, standing with Grandma "D." The crowd rose to their feet and began to chant: "She is the champion…"

Tears ran down Grandma "D"'s cheeks. Jason handed her the picture. Her hands shook as she read the inscription:

Grandma "D"—I will never be able to repay you for all you have done for me. I thank you for the respect you gave me when I first came to your home. Because of that giving, you taught me to respect myself and others. In return, I have been respected amongst my peers and have excelled beyond my childhood imaginations! Love for eternity—Jason

Grandma "D" looked up. She raised the picture for all to see. The hockey players skated around the arena, Jason leading the way, skating backwards so he would not miss a moment of the joyous expression upon her face. Having gone full circle, the team stopped at the main exit.

Jason reached out his arms, into which his team-mates gently placed Grandma "D." He leaned over and whispered: "Let's go home."

She glanced into his misty eyes, smiled and said: "Let's," as she reached up a knurled finger and wiped the tears from his cheeks.

Grandma's Apron

Alexis turned onto the walkway that led up to her grandma's house. She opened the front door. The hinges creaked with age.

"Grandma!"

The furniture looked unusually dusty.

"In the kitchen, dear."

Her grandma was sitting in an old rocker by her stove. There was a chair beside her. "Sit down, dear, I have something for you. Would you mind pouring me a cup of tea first—get yourself a drink, too."

Drinks in hand and back in the chair, Alexis asked, "What's up, Grandma?"

Her grandma placed a package on Alexis' lap. "Open it, love."

Alexis opened the package and felt a twinge of disappointment when all she saw was her grandma's tattered old apron. The elderly woman sensed her granddaughter's disenchantment.

"That apron belonged to my mother."

"Even worse than I imagined," Alexis thought.

"It will be easier to tell its story if you put the apron on, dear."

Alexis humoured her grandmother. The story began the moment she tied the bow…

"My mother made this apron from a piece of cotton her mother gave her. She was told an apron would be one of her most valuable tools in life. Oh, I am sure my mother might have laughed inside, as did I when it was passed to me, and as did your mother when I gave it to her.

Unfortunately, with your mother's untimely passing, this legacy has been returned to me to pass on to you.

"Now, for the story ... listen carefully, because one day you will pass this on to your child. The original fabric was bright red—hard to see now because of all the patches—but, there is a story for every swatch, as well.

"See this blue teardrop shaped one in the corner ... that's the one that was used to dry my mother's tears, mine and your mother's. Touch it, see if you can feel the tears in the cloth."

Alexis was surprised, the patch felt damp.

"Even dried a few of your tears, dear."

Alexis remembered.

"See this patch ... this was from my mother's Sunday go-to-meeting dress. It covered a hole where the material burned through when my mother was taking a hot pot from the oven in the wood cook stove. I remember the terrible burn on her hand too."

Grandma sipped her tea. "In the early mornings, we'd go out to the chicken coop; mother would hold the apron. I'd gather, and then set the eggs in it. Sometimes, we would have to bundle the hatchlings up in the apron on a frigid winter day, before taking them up to the house so that they wouldn't freeze."

Grandma began to ramble...

"In the summer, when the men were in the fields, mother would ring the dinner bell and then wave her apron so they would know she was calling them for a meal, not an emergency ... see this patch ... it is from an old pair of curtains that used to hang in our sitting room. A piece of kindling ripped a hole there ... your mother was so shy she used to hide behind my apron whenever we had company

... I used to play peek-a-boo with you ... you liked this patch the best."

Grandma pointed to a piece of white material with red polka-dots. "That was one of your mother's Sunday dresses. It covers a hole from a downward pointing squash stem...

"See this one," grandma pointed to the opposite corner from the teardrop patch. "My mother used this one to wipe her brow; one side for sweat and one side for tears, she would say."

Grandma finished her cup of tea. The cup rattled as she set it on the saucer. Alexis noticed the pain flirt through the old eyes. "Your grandpa always surprised me with unexpected company. It was a Saturday night, and the house was a mess after a busy week of canning, and he gave me only a half hour notice that he was bringing his boss home for supper. Besides cooking extra food, I gave the furniture a good dusting with the apron. See this piece––it was from grandpa's favourite shirt––I used that to hide the tear I put in the apron when it got caught on a nail on the side of the buffet as I was dusting that day."

Alexis learned how her mother used to pick fruit and carry them in grandma's apron ... she learned how grandma used to wrap her mom up in the warm apron when she came in from school on cold, rainy days ... she learned how, one day, a hired hand had ridden one of her great-grandfather's horses too hard, and the apron had been used to rub the horse down ... she learned, most of all that this apron was a valuable piece of her family history.

Grandma sat back in her rocker. Her eyes closed.

"Grandma, before I leave, would you like me to help you up to bed?"

"No child, I just want to sit a bit longer."

As Alexis walked home, her tears began to pour. She lifted the teardrop patch to her eyes, and so began the stories of the next generation.

Oh, Henry

Even though it would be a long walk for someone who was 90, Edna had insisted on being dropped off at the end of the lane. She assured Tina she would be fine; she had her cane. She instructed Tina to return, up to the house, in an hour. Edna was positive, by then, she would have found what she was looking for.

"Wherever is Jeffrey?" Edna mumbled as she shuffled along. "He used to take such good care of the grounds. Lazy old so and so, letting all these weeds grow up in my flower beds." Edna paused at the front door. "What a fool I am; Jeffrey must be dead," she laughed. "He was fifty when I left here sixty years ago. Where is my mind?"

Edna entered the dimly lit foyer and made her way to the den. As she stepped through the doorway, she sensed something was different. Even though she had not set foot on the old homestead for sixty years, her last memories, of this room in particular, were as dark and eerie as the shadows before her now.

Her cane made a tapping sound on the wooden floor. A tattered carpet almost tripped Edna as she passed by the Victorian couch. Scuttling in the far corner startled her—maybe a mouse. Henry had made Edna get rid of her cats—he hated cats. Of course, just as she had warned him, the house became overrun with mice. "Even then, you wouldn't let me get a cat, would you, Henry?" Edna declared.

Her hand brushed against the old armoire. She shuddered. "Oh, Henry, why did you turn so mean?" Edna laughed hysterically. "There was not much time, and I had a breakdown; completely mad they declared me—still am, they think—that is why I've been locked up all these years." Edna's face took on a faraway look. "Poor dear, they all said, he just left her; what a scoundrel that Henry!"

Edna looked around. Her eyes were beginning to adjust to the dim light in the room. She glanced at the watch on her wrist. Tina would be along soon with the car to take her back to that place she was supposed to call home. "Oh, dear, the armoire has been moved," she whispered.

It had not been in the middle of the room when she had last seen it. She ambled to the picture window. The familiar red curtains, though faded and covered with dust, still hung from the brass rod. It had been an advantageous colour for the events of that night. The carpet was red too.

Edna fumbled about for the drawstring. She was going to need two hands to pull these across. She set her cane against the wall and tugged. The curtains squeaked open. Dust floated to the floor. Edna swayed with the dancing particles. She hummed her favourite song, "You Light Up My Life." The one she used to sing for Henry—the one she still sang for him.

Edna retrieved her cane and continued her slow dance. She lovingly touched the wallpaper. "Yes, here it is——the mural! Just where I put it. Such a lovely waterfall. Such a beautiful mountain." Edna smiled. "Oh, Henry, you promised me we'd retire up there in our very own log cabin. I couldn't find a mural with a log cabin, though."

Edna heard the front door open. "Tina, is that you, dear?"

Tina entered the den. "Is everything okay, Mrs. Jones?"

"Oh, yes."

"Do you mind telling me what you are looking for?" Tina walked over and put her arm around Edna.

"I guess I can, it doesn't matter anymore, anyway. I was looking for Henry."

"Oh, you poor dear, how could you think you'd find Henry here after all these years? You know he disappeared without a trace sixty years ago. Come along Mrs. Jones; I think you've had enough excitement for one day; I should never have brought you here."

A mysterious smile spread across Edna's face. "I know they never found him, dear," she said. "You know, Henry always wanted to be buried on our mountain by the waterfall." She laughed as she caressed the mural and then rambled on. "How are you, Henry? Remember how nice you were when we were first married? But then you changed, and you were so mean, and I kept warning you—didn't I, Henry? I knew they'd never find you here!"

"I beg your pardon, Mrs. Jones?"

"Oh, Henry, my love, I warned you not to make me get rid of my cats!"

Tina fainted.

Edna was tired. She ambled over to the wooden rocker in the corner and sat down. She smiled and hummed Henry's song. Tina would wake up soon and take her home. Everything here was in order. Henry was where he had always wanted to be.

Precious Boxes

Caroline looked around her new home. There was a warmth within that she had never felt in any other place she'd lived. Shadows of picture frames were scattered randomly on the walls. Marks on a doorframe measured the yearly growth of children who had once lived here. The odd forgotten memento had been left behind—a landscape of the 'old country' on the rec room wall, an old box radio in the kitchen, an arrangement of plastic flowers on the bathroom counter, aluminum pots in the basement kitchen, a couple dozen crown canning jars in the fruit cellar…

Caroline headed to the basement, to the room that had brought tears to her eyes the first time she'd come through the house. She stepped through the doorway and was surprised to see the boxes were still there against the walls, and above each one, was an envelope with a name on it. Caroline was puzzled as to why no one had come for them before the closing date.

The name above the first box was Julie. Caroline wondered what was inside. She reasoned that technically everything here belonged to her as she stuck her hand inside. Her fingers met with a soft material. Within was a stunning, handmade, patchwork quilt. Caroline lifted it out. She could tell by the pieces of fabric that it was old, yet the colours had remained vibrant—it had been well looked after. She reached for the envelope. Maybe there was an address inside; maybe Julie just didn't know this was here.

The note had been written by a very shaky hand…

Dear Julie—I know how you always loved this quilt when you used to come for sleepovers. I always enjoyed it when you sat on my knee and asked me where each one of the squares come from. Maybe one day you can pass it on to one of your granddaughters. Love, Grandma

Caroline moved on to the next box. Inside was a figurine of a male ballet dancer. On the envelope was the name, Philip.

Dear Philip—I am so happy you never gave up your dream of dancing. I know how difficult it was for you; I saw the way some children treated you. I found this at a flea market and thought of you—hope you like it. Love Grandma

The next box contained a set of old cookbooks for Emily.

Dear Emily—these are the cookbooks I was given when I was a new bride. I always enjoyed your eagerness to learn how to cook when you visited. Love Grandma
p.s. I've marked our special recipes with a red sticker heart.

A sculptured face of an elderly lady lay in the next box. It was for Karen.

Dear Karen—I am returning this to you. I remember the day you gave it to me—I loved it, but you cried because you didn't think it was a good likeness of me. Show it to your children and grandchildren, so they will know what I looked like way back when. Love Grandma

Caroline spent the next half hour going through numerous boxes that held small mementos for friends. Finally, she came to the last one: Maria's. Inside were several old photo albums and some timeworn letters—also a package of lined paper and a pen.

Dear Maria—I know there are stories inside of your heart that you wish to write. I thought my letters and the photos in these albums might be the right place to start. I have tried, where I could remember, to mark down names, dates and locations. The rest you can either make up or

*check with some of the aunts and uncles who are still
around. I know you will do a fantastic job—you have your
father's love of the written word—use it well; follow your
dream. Love Mamma*

There were no addresses anywhere.

Caroline wiped the tears from her eyes. These
boxes did not belong to her. She went upstairs and
retrieved her real estate agent's card. Caroline had bought
the home as part of an estate sale—everything had gone
through a lawyer.

"Good morning, Doug's Realty, how might I direct
your call?"

"Sheila Turner, please."

"One moment."

"Sheila here…"

"Hi, this is Caroline. I found some things in the
house that I believe belong to the family. Do you know how
I can reach them?"

"I'll see what I can find out and get back to you."

Three months passed. Caroline had settled into her
new home quite nicely. One day, Caroline noticed a
middle-aged woman staring at the house. "May I help you?"
she asked.

"I'm Maria … this was my mother's house," a
hesitant smile was on her face.

"Do come in," Caroline opened the door wide. "I've
been keeping some boxes for you and your children."

Saying Goodbye to Wally

Muriel and Florence had been friends for a long time. They were always together. Today was a sad day for them—one of many they'd been experiencing lately. Wally had passed away.

"He was only 93," Muriel said, tears in her eyes.

"Going to miss him," Florence sniffled. "But 93 isn't a bad life."

"But he was so healthy; this was so unexpected," Muriel blew her nose.

"Don't be silly; it's always expected at our age," Florence snorted. "I'm just thankful when I wake up in the morning and there's no chalk line around my body!"

The friends laughed.

"Ready?" Florence asked.

"Yep … let's go and say goodbye to Wally."

Florence still had her licence; she wasn't sure for how long though. At 89 her eyesight was starting to dim. She felt sorry for Muriel who'd lost her licence eight years ago when she'd turned 80.

Muriel and Florence sat eight seats from the front of the chapel—far enough back to not interfere with the family, but close enough to denote that their relationship was of an almost kinship nature. There weren't many people—who are left when you're 93? Family and friends—those who were still alive.

The organ began playing, "I've Got a Mansion." Muriel and Florence hummed along. That had been Wally's favourite hymn. The music finished, the mourners stood, and the funeral procession proceeded up the church aisle. Wally's two daughters, his son, and their families followed behind the casket—all of them dabbing at their eyes with crinkled tissues. Once seated, the minister said an opening prayer and then…

"Ecclesiastics talks about times: a time to be born … a time to die. Today, we are here to celebrate Wally's *times*. Wally was here a long time—93 years, but of course to those who love him as a father, grandfather, brother, uncle, friend—that is still too young to have to let him go.

"During this past month, as Wally's health began to fail, I was privy to some fantastic stories—too numerous to relate here today. He sure loved life!"

Muriel and Florence looked at each other, nodded and smiled.

"Wally told me," the pastor continued, "that recently, some of his best times were playing bridge at the senior's club. He said he'd made numerous friends there, and that there were so many beautiful women around that he hadn't wanted to get attached to any particular one for fear of affronting the others!"

The guests snickered. Muriel and Florence looked at each other, nodded, smiled and then returned their attention to the service.

"Wally loved soccer. He played, as a lad in Scotland; when he came to Canada, he coached young children for about 30 years. He even played in an old-timers league when he turned 35. Of course, as time passed, his body said no more, so he just did play by plays with whatever games he could watch on the tube."

Muriel and Florence looked at each other, nodded and smiled. They remembered some of Wally's "after game" barbecues! They weren't really interested in soccer, but Wally'd made great burgers!

"Most of all, though, Wally loved his family and friends. He showed me his picture albums, filled with memories of his life with Violet, his children, grandchildren and great-grandchildren. Scattered amongst those pictures were shots of his friends, from as early as his childhood in Scotland, to recent moments here in Brantford."

Muriel and Florence looked at each other, nodded and smiled. They had their own unique albums and Wally appeared in several of their photos.

"Remember the picture from the Christmas party?" Muriel whispered in Florence's ear.

Florence nodded and smiled.

"Wally pointed out several of his special photos, and he asked me to put a slide show together and play it for those who attended his funeral. He'd laughed and mentioned that if no one showed up, I could archive the memories to the library for some future generations to laugh at!"

Muriel and Florence looked at each other, nodded and smiled.

For the next 15 minutes, the guests watched pieces of Wally's life flick across the screen. There were smiles, tears, giggles, and outright laughter at times. Muriel and Florence kept looking at each other, nodding, smiling, sometimes laughing, sometimes dabbing at their eyes.

The ride home was quiet. Florence focused on the road. Once in a while, she would wipe her eyes. Muriel stared out the side window. Once in a while, she would dab at her nose with her handkerchief.

As they walked into their house, Florence broke the silence: "That was a beautiful picture of you, me, and Wally at his last barbecue, wasn't it?

"I loved the caption too—Wally and his favourite gals, Florence and Muriel."

The two friends looked at each other, nodded, smiled and then closed the door.

Shattered Dream

She rocks.
She hums.
She hopes.
She dreams.

The timeworn grandmother sits in her rocking chair, hoping and dreaming upon the fantasies in her mind. She hopes that one day her daughter will come and take her away from this place she is supposed to call home. She dreams that she is living her life within the solace of four walls, surrounded by her family—not in the confines of long, narrow hallways, crowded wards, noisy dining rooms and dimly lit sleeping quarters—surrounded by strangers. She hopes her daughter will at least visit her today. She hopes to see her grandchildren. As the rocking chair sways back and forth, her eyes close and she hums a funny little song. Her lips curl upwards into a crinkled smile and her dream begins.

Her dream begins with the early morning scramble of a young family. Grandma is having a cup of tea with her son-in-law. Her daughter is busy preparing her husband's lunch. The sounds of laughter and grumbling echo from the upstairs of the house—"I was in the bathroom first!"—"No, you weren't, I was." Such sweet music to a lonely, old grandmother's ears.

The baby cries; the young mother looks frustrated—so much to do, so little time to accomplish it all. Grandma struggles up from her chair, places a reassuring hand on her daughter's shoulder and says, "Just relax; I'll get the baby for you." Grandma rocks her newest granddaughter and hums a soft lullaby. "You look like me," she whispers to the infant. The baby gurgles contentedly. The grandmother sighs serenely. The chair rocks on. The baby sleeps. Grandma takes the infant and lays her gently in her crib.

"Good morning, Grandma. Would you brush my hair for me, please? Mommy is busy making our school lunches."

"Of course I will, sweetheart." And when grandma is finished, her reward is a kiss, a hug, and a murmured, "Thank you, Grandma; I love the way you do my hair."

The house becomes silent, the majority of the family leaves to meet the day's challenges. The baby sleeps on. Grandma sits down in the rocking chair and reaches for the pile of socks that have been waiting for months to be mended. Her daughter enters the room with an armful of laundry.

"Here, let me help you fold that," the elderly woman says to her daughter.

"It's okay, Mama. You relax."

"But I insist; I want to help."

"Well okay, but make sure you don't overexert yourself."

The day passes quickly for the busy grandmother. In the afternoon, while the baby is napping, she prepares a special treat for after the supper, and her daughter, free of children, manages to buy her groceries in half the usual time.

Before Grandma realizes, the grandchildren are home from school, her son-in-law is home from work, and they are all sitting down for a nice family meal. There is laughter and life around the table. There is talk of the day's events. After supper, Grandma reads a story to the children while her daughter tidies in the kitchen. Later, Grandma helps her son-in-law tuck the older children into bed while her daughter feeds the baby. The children have received extra story time, hugs, and kisses tonight because Grandma is there.

Peace descends on the home. The grandmother sits down, turns on the T.V., and looks over to her daughter, "Why don't you and your hubby go out for a couple of hours tonight and have some fun," she suggests. "The children are all sleeping, everything will be fine here."

On their way out the door, the young couple leans over and kiss the withered, old cheek. "Thanks, Mom, you're great. Where have you been all these years?"

The old woman's face crinkles into a thousand lines. Tears stream down her leathery cheeks and love flashes from the dampened eyes. "Oh, I've been around."

What a beautiful dream this is turning out to be for the aged grandmother. She is busy. She is useful. She has some control over her life. She is functioning in society again...

She rocks on...

She hums on...

She hopes on...

She dreams on...

The face of the "dream grandma" is so serene. Her lips remain firm in their crinkled smile...

"Come on, Annie, it's time for your medicine." The dream is shattered. Reality strikes as the nurse passes the old woman her pills. "I swear, Annie; you would sleep forever in this rocking chair if we let you."

"Then let me," Annie utters.

The Barn Wall

Sally sat on the edge of her bed, gazing around the room she had slept in for the past ten years. She had given up the large master bedroom when her daughter, Angel, married Mike. It had been the proper thing to do, and the room had produced three terrific grandchildren for her. However, the time had finally arrived for Sally to leave her home: she knew she soon would need constant care with the way her eyesight was failing.

Sally stood, walked over to the window and pulled the curtain across. The old green barn was fuzzy from this distance. She noticed some missing boards and knew it wouldn't be long before the entire barn would be gone. Then the memories it kept would vanish as well.

She glanced to the corral—empty now—closed her eyes and dreamed back to her first adventure there. She had been six, and her father thought it was time for her to learn to ride the farm pony. Sally smiled. The pony only cooperated for two rounds and then dumped her off. It was two years before she set foot in a stirrup after that experience.

"I did become a pretty good rider in the long run, though," Sally giggled as she let the curtain fall back into place. "Can't remember for the life of me what the name of that darn pony was!"

Sally ambled around the room. She inscribed her name, via fingertip, in the dust on the old walnut dresser. She didn't dare take it with her for fear someone besides family would snatch it. It was a family heirloom, passed to her mother, from her mother, and goodness knows from where—"I think you came from Scotland, didn't you, old friend?" Sally muttered to the dresser. "Held a lot of things for me over the years, some secrets too, didn't you?" She stroked the wood.

She began opening the drawers, double-checking for any left behind treasures she might have missed while packing. In the bottom drawer, she noticed a black and white photo that was almost ready to escape out the far back corner.

Sally retrieved the picture and stared at it longingly. She raised it to her mouth and breathed a soft kiss to the lips that smiled to her. She heaved a deep sigh as the photo misted over, then laid it gently in the still open suitcase on the bed. Sally took one more look around the room before she closed the lid and snapped it shut. There was just one more thing she had to do before leaving. She retrieved her cane from beside the nightstand and headed out the door.

The trek to the barn was slow for Sally. Her old bones didn't move as quickly as they had back when memories were vivid and the future was even brighter. She pushed open the barn's man door and stepped inside. The fragrant smell of hay was sweet to her nostrils.

"At least my sense of smell isn't going yet," she muttered as she closed the door.

Rays of sunlight forced their way through the cracks and into the barn. They would make Sally's task much more manageable. She made her way over to the *special* wall—the one where everyone had etched their love. *Arthur loves Maggie … George loves Betty … James and Donna Forever …* lots of hearts and arrows and stick people kissing. And there, right in the bottom left-hand corner, the inscription Sally was searching for: *Jonah and Sally, our love as soft as petals on a morning rose, as strong as steel upon the bridges of time, love forever, never forgotten!* Tears began to roll down Sally's withered cheeks.

She shook her head—that had been a terribly long time ago. Jonah was gone. In fact, Sally had no idea where he was; he just disappeared without a trace, without a word. Her heart never mended, but she had been forced to push onward with life. Now that she was departing from her home and her memories, Sally knew she must leave Jonah a note—just in case he returned.

She reached into her pocket and pulled out a red marker. Her arthritic fingers painstakingly began to print her message on the old barn wall.

Dear Jonah—if you do return like I have always dreamed you would, I want you to know I never stopped loving you. There is no one for me but you. I am waiting at the old folks' home, Paradise Acres, you know the one where we used to visit old Mr. Crabbit … I have a lovely room there … private, so we can be alone. I hope you can read this, my writing is so frail, but my mind is still sharp with the memories of our love. Don't be afraid to come … we have much to catch up on … love forever … never forgotten … your Sally.

P.S. our daughter—I named her Angel—is beautiful. We have three incredible grandchildren: Jonah, Jason, and Julia. I left some pictures for you in the box at our secret place … do you remember where … three steps to the left … one to the right … four forward from the old oak tree…

Sally returned the marker to her pocket, turned slowly and left the warmth of the old barn wall.

The Derby

Alex had spent hours working on his go-cart for the big race that was coming up on the weekend. He had gathered various pieces of wood from the barn and used old nails he had found to piece the wood together. There had been a tin of old green paint sitting on the shelf in the drive-shed, and he had mixed it with some turpentine to obtain just the right consistency to coat the go-cart. Another tin had just enough red paint in it to write *BLAZER* on each side. Alex had found an old tractor steering wheel and some old piping that he fashioned into wheel axles. He had stood back and admired his handiwork and was dreaming about crossing the finish line first. Everything was perfect—everything except that Alex had not been able to locate a set of wheels.

He had searched the farm high and low for a set of wheels. He had even asked some of his friends, but they were all working on their own go-carts and didn't have any to spare. Harold offered him one wheel, and then he smirked and walked away. Alex couldn't wait to cross the finish line and have Harold eat his dust!

As of Saturday morning, Alex still hadn't found a set of wheels. He rose early and went down to the barn and just sat there, staring at his beautiful go-cart. The sun was peeking through the cracks in the haymow and dust was dancing in the beams.

"I wish this were magic fairy dust," Alex mumbled. "And that I could be granted a set of wheels."

"Alex!" His mother called from the porch. "Alex, I need you to take Kenneth for a buggy ride."

Alex stood up and walked back to the house. "Oh well," he thought, "Next year."

His mom had his baby brother wrapped in a blanket in the big buggy. "Kenneth won't settle down and I need to get my baking done, or we won't have any bread. Take him down along the lake road until he falls asleep and when you bring him back, leave the buggy under the oak tree behind the house. Then you can get about your other chores. I'll hear him if he wakes up."

Alex was sullen as he pushed the buggy down the lane. What he should do is just push it over the edge into the lake. He hadn't asked for another brother, especially one he had to tend to on the day of the big race. And his mom didn't even realize that—she didn't care about what his plans were for the day!

The sound of the wheels calmed Kenneth. He stopped crying and was looking up at his older brother. Soon his eyes began to droop and then closed entirely. Alex wheeled the buggy back home and placed it under the oak tree. As he pushed his foot on the wheel-brake, he smiled! If Kenneth was asleep in the carriage, there was no need for it to have wheels!

Just then, Jimmy came around the corner of the house. "Jimmy, come here," Alex called out. Alex explained to his younger brother what he was about to do and what role he was to play. Jimmy was shaking his head, but then Alex drove home the words that closed the deal for him.

"You owe me, Jimmy. Remember the time I covered for you when you skipped school—actually if truth be told here, more than one time! This is extremely important to me!" Alex got busy with what he had to do. It was a good thing that Kenneth, once he fell asleep, was a sound sleeper.

It was a thrilling race. Alex was beside Harold in the starting line. They had glared at each other. Alex could see

Harold was not happy, especially when he saw the size of the wheels on Alex's go-cart. It had been a tight race. Harold was bigger and stronger than Alex, but in the end, it was the large buggy wheels that had given Alex the edge and pushed the nose of his go-cart over the finish line, just ahead of the rest of the pack. Harold had grudgingly shaken Alex's hand on the podium.

The first thing Alex saw as he was pedaling the go-cart up his laneway was his mom standing on the front steps with her hands on her hips. And the look on her face told him all was not well!

"Alex! You have some explaining to do, young man!"

Alex looked up at the second story window of the house, to where the bedroom he shared with Jimmy was. Jimmy was standing in the window—distress was written all over his face. "Oh well," Alex muttered under his breath as he gazed at the trophy he'd just won. Not even his mom's broom handle could ruin this day for him!

The Letter

Muriel wandered through the emptiness of her home. It had been six months since she last held his hand, walked with him in their garden, enjoyed a tea with him in their three-season room, or awakened to his smiling eyes as he informed her if she didn't get up, breakfast would be cold. Tears flowed shamelessly down Muriel's creviced cheeks.

"How foolish some women are," she mumbled as she entered the bathroom. "One day their man will be gone, and they won't have to complain about him leaving the seat up!" Muriel reached over and put the toilette seat down. It was something she did to keep his presence close. Finished, she raised the seat, washed her hands, and headed off to her empty bedroom.

She flipped on the T.V. and scrolled to channel five. "Good there is a ten o'clock news; I can't stay awake much past 10:30 anymore, even with all my daytime cat naps! Nothing but tragedies!" Muriel grumbled. "Well, not tonight … maybe I'll just read one of these dusty books."

Muriel turned the T.V. off, selected a novel from her bookshelf and crawled into bed. After ten minutes, she laid the book on her lap. Reading wasn't easy since he had gone away. She began to mull over the conversations at her great niece's wedding shower. "How foolishly some look at life," Muriel thought. "How can I change that for my niece?"

She stared into space, then smiled: "I'll give her a priceless wedding gift, the voice of reminiscence, and I'll pray my niece will embrace a different world from that of her naïve, tittering friends." Muriel shuffled over to her old oak roll top desk, retrieved paper and pen, then sat down to write a letter to her great niece.

Dear Tanya: It is with great love that I write this letter to you. First, I must say I enjoyed your wedding shower today. It was nice to see so much family together in one place— weddings and funerals are famous for such gatherings— but I need to discuss something of vital importance with you—your relationship with that young man, James, whom you are about to pledge a lifetime of love and devotion to before God and family. I eavesdropped on conversations today—you didn't realize I was nosey, did you? Well, I'm glad I am because now I can save you from some ill advice from your friends.

Love is a two-way street. When you wake up in the mornings, it is not all about what your partner can do for you, it is about what you can do for them—if you both think this way, selfishness will not creep into your day. It doesn't matter who makes the coffee or plugs in the tea kettle— what matters is that it gets done with a happy heart. It doesn't matter who clears the dishes off the table after a meal, or who sweeps the crumbs from the floor; who brings home the bacon, or who mows the lawn; who takes the car for an oil change, or who gets under the car's hood to tune it up. It doesn't matter who wakes in the night to walk a teething baby or who bandages a scraped knee, as long as it is done with love. There are so many things in life that don't matter, but what really does matter is that you each do what you are best at and then step up to the plate for everything else when necessary. Do not make a 'cut in granite' his and her list, for there may be a day when one of you cannot bandage the knee, or do the dishes, or go to work or mow the lawn—you get my drift, dear niece ... the advice I impart to you is to walk down life's road with your young man, side by side, and never allow the idiocy of outsiders to put a thorn into your love. Kiss each other good morning, goodnight, and several times throughout the day.

And lastly, dearest Tanya, don't worry if he leaves the toilet seat up—one day he may not be there to do that. Whatever will you do then! I wish for you as delightful a life as your Uncle James and I had. Love, Aunt Muriel

Muriel folded her letter, placed it in an envelope, sealed it and pressed a stamp on the corner. "I'll mail this in the morning," she said as she got up and went to lie down on her bed.

Tears streamed down Tanya's face as she read the letter. Her mom had found it on the old oak desk while sorting through Aunt Muriel's possessions after the funeral.

That evening, Tanya re-read the letter to James. "We should frame this and hang it in a special spot," James' voice was filled with emotion.

"I know just the place," Tanya replied. "On the wall at the front entrance, for everyone who enters our home to see."

"Perfect," said James as he leaned over and kissed his bride of two weeks.

Mom Will Never Know

A scorching breeze blew across the field. Jessica detested having to hoe the corn because the heat was so unbearable for her.

With her red hair and fair, freckled skin, Jessica's mom forced her to wear long-sleeved shirts, long pants, and a huge straw hat, even on the hottest of days. When she was younger, she hadn't cared much, but she'd be fourteen in the fall—an age far beyond having to dress so ridiculously.

Jessica noticed the dip in the field coming up. At that point, her mother would no longer be able to see her from the kitchen window, and she would be able to free herself from the heavy clothing and the ridiculous straw hat.

A meowing sound was heading towards Jessica. "Here kitty, kitty," she called. "I'm over here, Whiskers!"

Whiskers was Jessica's cat. He had been the runt of the litter and had never really grown much bigger than a six-month-old kitten. What he lacked in size though, he made up for in heart. The dog next door always chased the farm cats, but Whiskers was the only cat who stood up to him. Of course, he made sure there was a good stout wall behind him when he gave Rufus the "what for" with his claws. Rufus was a real bully, always backing down when challenged.

Jessica hoed a few more feet of corn before Whiskers reached her. He rubbed around her legs, purring loudly. She leaned over and patted the top of his head.

"Can't pick you up till we get a bit further; don't want mom to see me slackin'."

Whiskers ran up the row chasing a bug, then plopped himself in the shade of a giant weed and waited.

Jessica glanced back towards the house and then hoed vigorously until she reached the dip.

"Need a good rain," she stated to Whiskers as the dust flew up from her hoe. "Can't understand how the weeds get so big in this heat," she mumbled. Jessica took a swig of water from her bottle. She cupped some in her hand and knelt down beside Whiskers. "Here you go," she offered.

Whiskers lapped up the water, then gave Jessica's fingers an extra licking. He purred, plopped over and demanded a belly rub. "Break time, eh?" she said as she complied with his wishes.

Jessica pulled the hat from her head and stripped off the long-sleeved flannel shirt, exposing her arms and shoulders to the sun. She had come prepared today, wearing a tank top under the big shirt. She rolled up her pant legs, and folded the shirt and placed it on top of the hat.

"There, we'll get this on our way back to the house," she informed Whiskers. "Mom will never know!"

For the next hour, Jessica enjoyed her freedom from the weighty clothes. She sang as she hoed. She could feel the sun on her bare skin, and she marvelled at how great it felt. Whiskers followed her up and down the rows, only leaving her once to catch a mole, which he promptly returned with and dropped at her feet.

Jessica glanced at her watch. Four-thirty—almost supper time. She stopped at her hat and shirt, sat down and unrolled her pants. Her legs were warm and pinkish in colour. She slipped into the flannel shirt and fastened the buttons. The material felt rough on her skin. Finally, she plopped the hat on her head, tied the string and headed home.

"Come on, Whiskers," Jessica called out. "Do you want a ride?" She said, scooping him up into her arms. He didn't resist. It had been a long, hot afternoon.

Jessica put the hoe in the garden shed. Her face felt very flushed. She also seemed a bit dizzy but passed it off as not having had enough water to drink. Whiskers raced off to the cool barn where he knew he would find a bucket of cold water.

"Mom!" Jessica called as she entered the kitchen.

"Jessica!" her mom shouted, "What have you done?"

Jessica was puzzled at her mom's welcome. "What do you mean?—I've been hoeing corn all afternoon," she replied.

"Did you take your hat off?"

"Occasionally, to wipe my brow," Jessica fibbed.

"Your face is beet-red," her mom exclaimed, "don't try and tell me that is from an occasional taking off of your hat!"

"Well it is dreadfully hot out," Jessica floundered. Her entire body was burning up now.

"Not that hot—your nose wouldn't be blistering so badly if your hat had been on!"

"My hat was on!" she yelled. "Why don't you believe me?" She stormed out of the kitchen, rushed to her room, slammed the door shut and stripped the flannel shirt off.

Jessica's shoulders drooped. "Oh, my God!" she cried as she looked in the mirror and saw her skin boiling with large white bubbles! "I'll never be able to hide these!"

Two Wedding Days

Ali raised Samira's hand to his lips and tenderly kissed her fingers. "Not a bad life we've had; who would have thought we'd last so long?"

Samira smiled knowingly. "Yes, who would have thought; definitely not my mother!"

"Nor mine!" Ali laughed.

"Fifty years," Samira sighed. "How nice of our children to arrange such a wonderful party."

"They are good children, like their mother," Ali said.

Ali and Samira celebrated their anniversary one week before the actual vows had been taken. Everyone knew the story, especially their children, who heard the tale every year.

"I'm not sure if I should have forgiven you, Ali," Samira stated. "My mother told me to forget you and marry someone else."

"My mother wouldn't speak to me for two days, and when she did, she said I would be lucky if you would still marry me!"

Samira laughed, "Your mother was right—you are lucky that I still married you; no other woman would have!"

Ali feigned a hurt look, "But it was the semi-final, and I had no choice; I thought you would understand!"

"What I understand is you left me at the altar on our wedding day. My mother had worked for days to prepare for our wedding feast. Our guests consoled your weeping bride, and then took food home with them so it wouldn't be wasted. Your mother didn't speak to you for two days—my mother cried for three!"

"It was a great game though; I wish you'd been there," Ali ventured on. "I know the money was for my wedding shoes, but when Omar called and said they didn't have a ball for the semi-final game, I had to do something!"

"You would have been better to buy the ball and show up to our wedding in your bare feet!"

Ali was a glutton for punishment. "Oh, Samira, my love—my life—if you had only seen the game. The new ball was magic. Our passes were perfect and when we shot at the net—well, you know our score was the talk of the village for months afterwards! And they needed me to play sweeper when Clovis became ill so suddenly."

"Oh yes, I remember, 8 – 0, a very high score for a soccer game. But George could have played that position," Samira informed her husband.

"George had a pulled thigh muscle, and there is no way he could have handled the sweeper position." Ali straightened his shoulders. "The original game was stormed out and we had to play before Wednesday. When a field became available for the Saturday … it was out of my hands!"

Samira would not accept excuses, even after fifty years. "You did wrong, Ali. Admit it!"

"And God punished me when our team lost the final!"

Samira laughed. "Actually, I've never seen you play such a bad game, before or since!"

Ali hung his head. "I wonder what happened to the ball; it disappeared after the game. In the championship, I felt disoriented without it!"

"I thought you played poorly because of all the reprimands you were given!" Samira offered up the real reason for Ali's lack of performance.

Ali smiled, "You are probably right, my love; how foolish to think a ball could actually help win a game!"

The couple cuddled closer. Despite the fact Samira had never let Ali forget what he had done, they'd had a beautiful life together. Their children had all played soccer and Ali still played in an old-timer's league.

And, in fifty years, Ali had never missed a family function because of a soccer match—unless Samira gave him permission, which she occasionally tended to do. She understood how much her husband loved the thrill of the game! After all, even against her mother's wishes and the advice of family and friends, she had still married him. Samira smiled as she pictured her young Ali, the brilliant executioner upon the soccer fields.

Ali checked his watch—seven-thirty. "I believe there is a World Cup game on now, Samira; would you like to watch it with me?"

"That would be nice."

Ali was so absorbed in the soccer game he didn't realize Samira left the room. When she returned, she handed him a gift bag. "Happy anniversary," she smiled.

Inside the bag was a soccer ball with names written on it. A note was taped to the ball. His face broke into a huge smile. "How?"

"Read the note."

My dear husband—if you are receiving this gift today, it is our 50th anniversary. My mother said we wouldn't last a year; your mother gave us six months. I told them that on our 50th anniversary I would present you with the ball which you won the game with on our wedding day. My greatest wish is for our mothers to live to see that day.
Love always and forever—your Samira
p.s. Just in case you were wondering how I got the ball—I convinced Clovis to give it to me!

Ali's heart burst with love for Samira, who had been his rock all these years—despite having left her at the altar on their first wedding day while he played a game of soccer!

Old John

Old John stood in the shadows of the boxcars, watching warily for those who would shoo him away before he could climb into one of the empty boxes. He had this down to a science now, but it had taken years of practice.

His clothes were ragged, patched together with twine and pins and needles. His shoes were holier than a sieve, and the feet inside them were bare and leathery. His grey hair was tied back into a ratted ponytail that straggled halfway down his back. A battered and dusty hat shadowed his weathered, dirt-streaked face. He chewed on a piece of straw—his meagre stash of cigarette stubs was to be saved for later, when no one would notice the smoke.

Old John was going nowhere in particular. He had come from nowhere in particular. He just followed the tracks wherever they led … to new towns … temporary towns that provided transitory jobs—sometimes. And then it was back into another boxcar … on the move again … along the lines … seeing the countryside through the open boxcar door.

The resolute rhythm of the wheels upon the steel rails would lull him into dreams, and he would dream of the times that used to be, and then of what might be around the next bend—perhaps a better world. He never dreamed of the present because he was living that.

There were many others like himself that Old John had met over the years. Some were still around, however many had just disappeared. A couple of them he truly missed because they had travelled numerous rails together. But that was the nature of the life he was destined to live—the way of the tracks.

Old John heard the familiar far-away whistle. He could feel the pulse of the railway lines through the soles of his shoes. His body tensed. His eyes were vigilant. He chewed harder on the straw and then spit the broken pieces on the ground. He knew that the train would only slow down at this station today because there was nothing to pick up or drop off—he had heard the station people talking. The whistle was ear-splitting, warning people to get off the track as the engine chugged slowly through the station. Old John finally saw what he was looking for—an open door. He checked the platform; the workers were joking around. What Old John would have given to have a job like that right now.

He moved quickly, nimbly for a man of his age, and leapt into the boxcar, settling in a shadowy corner—that was best until the train was well out of the station. Then he could come out and sit nearer the window of his world—even swing his feet out into the summer breezes.

"Howdy there, Old John," a voice from the opposite corner whispered gruffly.

Old John adjusted his eyes to the darkness. He smiled. Hank. It was going to be a pleasant trip. He hadn't seen Hank for a long time. "Hey there, Hank, how you been you old buzzard?"

"Gettin' too old fer this … almost couldn't get m'self up here this time … maybe I'll just stay here, till they finds me … hopefully not till we're on the open prairie though … that's where I was born, ya know … that's where I wants to be buried."

"Didn't know that." Old John hunkered down. "Better be quiet till we get out of here."

As the train left the city and headed into the open countryside, Old John and Hank came out of their corners. Old John handed Hank a cigarette stub. "Got a match?"

Hank dug around in his pockets. The two old chaps sat on the edge of the boxcar, their feet dangling over the edge, the wind whipping at their flimsy clothing. They waved to some children in a field. The children ran along beside the tracks as fast as they could, for as far as they could, before disappearing from view.

"Hope they will never have to ride the train like us; hope they will be able to pay for their tickets," Old John said.

"Heck, they'll miss half the world stuck in one of those fancy cars," Hank snorted.

"Guess you're right, but it's a tough world we live in."

"Tough, but I wouldn't have it no other way, Old John. Been the best years of my life, despite the hardships." Hank drew heavily on the last dregs of his smoke.

There was a silence between the two men as the world sped past them. Night crept in around them, and they curled up in opposite corners. As the sun came creeping into the boxcar, Old John stretched his legs and then stood up. "Hank, it's morning … wake up … we should be pulling into another station soon." He walked over to the doorway. "Hey there Hank … look at this … the Prairie … Hank … you lazy old so and so … wake up!"

Old John walked over to his friend, knelt down and touched him on the shoulder. It was cold—colder than would be normal after a chilly night in a boxcar. He placed a finger under Hank's nostrils. Not a flutter. "Well, Hank," Old John stood up. "I guess you got yer wish."

The sun burst into the boxcar just as the whistle blew its announcement that the train was entering the station. The engines began to slow down. Old John knew the train would stop here. He took one last look at his friend. "I guess you're home, Hank," he mumbled, and then jumped from the train and walked toward the station. This didn't look like too big of a town—probably no jobs here, especially for someone his age. Old John would just hang around in the shadows for a while until he decided where he wanted to go next. The rails would tell him—they always did.

Too Late

It was a sobering moment for the family as they gathered in the hospital, waiting for the doctor to deliver the news. "He is such a good boy," the woman with the greying hair cried softly into an older man's shoulder.

He, in turn, patted her gently on the back. "Yes, he is Carla, but he shouldn't have been doing what he was doing."

"I know," the words choked from her throat. Carla pulled out of her husband's arms and slumped into a chair in the corner of the waiting room. She glanced over to her daughter, Stacey, who was staring out the window. Stacey would be 16 this year. She was already chomping at the bit to get her driver's licence. Carla would have to speak to Bob about delaying that part of their daughter's life. "If only I'd told him he couldn't go to the party," she muttered.

Bob heard what she said. "It wouldn't have mattered," he sat down beside his wife. "If it weren't this party, it would have been the next. Randy should have known better. How many times have we told him not to drink and drive—to call a taxi, or to give us a call if there was no other way home? There is no one to blame here but Randy. *He* got behind the wheel—we didn't put him there!" Bob added angrily.

"Maybe he did call and we were so fast asleep we didn't hear the phone," Carla excused her son's not calling.

"Highly unlikely," Bob stated matter-of-factly. He hated it when his wife tried to defend the children against better judgement. She was too soft. "I'm going for a coffee; you want something?"

"No, thanks. I couldn't eat or drink anything right now."

"How about you, Stacey?"

Stacey shook her head and continued staring out the window. She was in her own world of torment at the moment. Randy was two years older than her, and she remembered the day he had come home with his G-1 licence. He'd been so excited and had told her that he could give her rides to school and to her friends—they wouldn't have to bother Mom or Dad so much. They had talked about never jeopardizing their lives, or that of their friends travelling in their car, by not drinking when they were the designated driver for the night. Randy had smiled and told her she would be able to get her licence soon, and that was something she should adhere too as well when she did.

She was angry at her brother because she also remembered the number of times lately that she had caught him coming in late at night, driving home from a party and had watched him stagger up to his room. And when she confronted him with that fact the next day, he would tell her to grow up and quit acting like a baby. "I wasn't drunk," he always said, and then he would mention to her that she should keep her mouth shut and not tell Mom and Dad or he wouldn't be running her around to her friends anymore and she would have to start taking the bus to school again. And as these thoughts raced through Stacey's mind, she became angry with herself at the selfishness she had shown. Her brother might not be in intensive care right now if she'd spoken up. And his friend Josh might not be in the morgue!

A month passed. Randy was coming home from the hospital. There had been several renovations that had had to be made to the family home. The news had been delivered a couple of days after the accident that Randy would never walk again. He would most likely regain the use of most of his upper body with extensive physiotherapy, but from the waist down, he would be totally paralyzed. Plus, not only would he be going to physiotherapy, but Randy would also be receiving counselling for drug and alcohol abuse. The doctors had found a high concentration of illegal substances in his blood the night of the accident. It was a very different young man who was wheeled up to the ramp to his home on that morning from the one who had driven home drunk and high a month earlier.

From across the street, Josh's mother parted the curtains and watched the procession. Another batch of tears escaped her eyes—some for the son she had just buried—some for the young man, his best friend, who would have to live the rest of his life with the guilt of what he had done!

Candy

The article in the newspaper had been tucked in a corner on the back page, but Dr. Kemp noticed it!

YOUTH FOUND DEAD IN MOTEL ROOM
Candy Malone, 18, was found dead in a motel room on West 7ᵗʰ St. on New Year's Day. The police had been beckoned when the motel owner called, saying he hadn't seen the girl for a couple of days. The phone receiver was off its hook—possibly an attempt to get help. From paraphernalia found at the scene, it appears drugs and alcohol may have been the cause of death. An autopsy will be performed to confirm the exact...

Dr. Kemp wondered if Candy had been trying to reach him. He rested his head in his hands, and his mind wandered back to December 27 when Candy had walked into his office...

Upon first sight, Candy had captured his heart. She had the face of a tormented angel.

"Come in please," he'd directed.

She'd hesitated before entering and then had curled up in the corner of the couch, as far from him as possible. When the "small talk" was out of the way, he had gotten right to the point: "When did it all fall apart, Candy?"

"Can't rightly say; it's been so long." Her voice was barely audible. "Maybe I should just go; I don't even know why I came here."

"A cry for help?"

"I'm beyond help."

"No one is beyond help, Candy. Why don't you start by telling me about your childhood."

"Childhood? Let me see, my parents constantly argued. After dad lost his job, he was either stoned or drunk. He'd beat my mom, and if my brother or I got in the way, we were beaten too. I tried to protect my little brother. It was a happy day when mom showed dad the door!"

"How old were you?"

"Seven."

"Your brother?"

"Four."

"Did things improve after that?"

"Not for long—Mom brought the boyfriend home. He was nice—at first. Then he..." Candy's lips had pursed angrily.

"He what?"

"Thought he owned me and could do whatever—by the time I was ten, he'd extended that ownership! It was hell. He threatened to do the same to my brother if I told my mom, so I kept silent. One of my teachers noticed how withdrawn I was, so she started questioning me. Finally, I told her. My mom wouldn't believe the social worker—she took his word over mine! Go figure, eh?" Candy had been visibly angry.

"Is that when you started drinking and using drugs?"

"Yeah, I guess. At first, it made me feel so good. The more I drank, the more I could block out. I would just curl up in a corner with my bottle and obliterate my world. "After all, isn't that what people do in the movies?"

"Movies aren't real though, Candy."

"Are you sure about that?" Candy was shaking.

He'd agreed with her that some T.V. shows used alcohol as a "fix-it tonic;" or portrayed it as the "fun and good times choice," primarily geared to youth.

"Then a friend introduced me to marijuana—that helped even more—I had so much to handle—it made everything go away—at the time…"

He'd pointed out that drugs were not a remedy; they were just an escape from learning positive coping mechanisms.

Dr. Kemp changed the subject. "What about boys?"

Candy had shrugged her shoulders. "Ha! Boys? Little men—had no problem fulfilling their needs—I'd been taught well! Good way to pay for my booze and drugs too—most of the time we just hung out and got stoned or drunk. Not much different from some of the adult parties I've been to, but I guess age gives them the right, eh? More adults should practice what they preach!"

Dr. Kemp couldn't have agreed more with her, yet how could he fix her damage? She'd had her youth ripped from her by those who should have loved and protected her. Only God knew what else she might be hiding, he'd thought at the time.

Candy had stood up. "I have to go now; gotta meet my brother. He's in a foster home, and I haven't seen him for a while. Everyone assumes I'm a bad influence on him."

"I'd like to talk to you again, Candy. May I book an…"

"I'll call you, doctor—I really must run." She headed for the door, but before leaving, she turned back. There had been an emptiness in her eyes that would haunt Dr. Kemp for a long time. "Thanks for tryin', Doc—you're okay." And then, she was gone.

Dr. Kemp leaned back in his chair. The newspaper fell to the floor. His shoulders shook as the dam in his heart released.

The Waiting Room

Elsie wondered if the plant on the coffee table was real. The layer of dust on the leaves indicated it might not be. Country music played in the background. A little boy was sitting on a chair, totally absorbed in his hand-held game system. Elsie had an hour to kill while her daughter was in with the councillor. She picked up a *Chatelaine* and began to read.

Every once in a while, the boy would shout excitedly and then he would glance Elsie's way. Elsie kept reading but watched him from the corner of her eye. All of a sudden, the boy was standing beside her. "I beat my mom and dad," he informed her. "I cleared this level—want to see?"

"Okay."

He showed her his score. Then he showed Elsie his mom and dad's scores. It didn't look like their scores were any different than his. However, she didn't say so; she just nodded and told him that it was awesome.

"Do your mom and dad play much?" she asked.

"They've only played once," he answered. He showed Elsie the next level he had to clear and then returned to his chair. Elsie resumed her reading. Shouts of victory informed her of the play by play on his progress. "I made it!" He looked over at Elsie. "Do you want to try it?"

"No, it's okay; you play—I don't really play games like that."

"You don't?"

"No."

The boy dug into the satchel on the chair beside him and pulled out another game. "Maybe you would like to try this one," he smiled.

"What is that one?" Elsie asked.

"Deal or No Deal."

"No, it's okay; you play." Elsie was trying hard not to sound irritated; she really just wanted to finish reading her magazine article.

The boy gathered up his belongings and brought them over to the chair beside Elsie. He made himself comfortable and then opened the game to show her how to play. "You pick a number," he pointed to all the numbered briefcases on the screen.

"Number 5," Elsie said.

This continued until she finished choosing all the allowed briefcases. The boy said she was doing really well, pointing out that the lower dollar amounts were better than the higher ones. Elsie asked him why. He explained, but she still didn't understand. "Oh well," she thought to herself; "it doesn't really matter."

"Now you have to say whether you want to make a deal with the bank or not," he looked up at Elsie with a smile. "The bank is offering you $28,000. You can make the deal and take that home, or you can say no and see what is in your briefcase."

"What do you think I should do?"

His eyes lit up. "I would make the deal; that is a lot of money!"

"Okay, deal then." Elsie's eyes roved over her magazine page.

"Oh, no!" he cried. "You would have had $320,000 if you hadn't made the deal!"

"But you told me to."

He giggled. "Want to play a game by yourself?"

Elsie gave up on her magazine. She returned it to the coffee table. Under the astute tutelage of the boy, she made it through an entire game and took home another $28,000; however, she missed out on the $720,000 she would have had, had she not made the deal!

"What's your name?" the boy asked.

"Elsie. What's yours?"

"Dallas."

"How old are you, Dallas?"

"Seven."

"What grade are you in?"

"Grade two."

"Do you like school?"

"No."

"Why not?"

"There aren't enough recesses."

A teenage boy entered the room and took a seat. "Do you want to play?" Dallas asked him.

The teenager smiled. "No, thanks."

"But it's fun!"

"That's okay; you play."

However, Dallas dragged him into the game. "Should I make the deal? $32,000 is a lot of money!"

"No."

"I want to."

"No way, man—don't make the deal!"

This banter continued. Dallas kept asking the teenager, and together they moved up the ladder of money. Dallas' mom entered the waiting room. She looked concerned. "I hope my son hasn't been bothering you?"

"On the contrary," Elsie replied; "he is very entertaining."

Dallas' mom sighed with relief. Dallas stood up and reached his hand to Elsie. "It was nice meeting you."

"It was nice to meet you too," Elsie replied. And then he was gone.

Elsie checked her watch; her daughter should be out in a few minutes. She had forgotten all about the plant and whether or not it was real—it was of no consequence. The most authentic part of her day had been Dallas, with his bright smile and warm heart.

Sophie's Christmas

Sophie leaned back in her rocking chair and sighed heavily. It was going to be another lonely Christmas. Harold had been gone for ten years, and her three children were scattered around the world. They hadn't been to visit in the past five Christmases—in fact, she hadn't even heard from any of them for months. Sometimes she wondered if they had forgotten her and all that she had ever done for them.

The intercom system announced a carol-sing in the activity room. Typically, Sophie attended the activities, but not today. She glanced out her window; it was starting to snow—light flakes floating down—winter finally getting his grip. She pulled a coverlet from her bed and tucked it around her legs. She was always cold lately.

"You not coming to the carol-sing?" a raspy voice questioned.

Sophie looked up and saw Charlie. He kept trying to get her *special attention*. "Don't feel like it today," she replied as politely as she could.

"I'll miss you."

"Then miss me." Sophie turned back to her window. Charlie shuffles away. "One man in my life was enough for me," she mumbled. She pressed the play button on her CD player, leaned back in her rocker and closed her eyes.

Carla picked up the phone and called her twin brother, Lance. She hoped he would agree with her plan. Their younger sister, Renee, had been difficult to convince, but eventually she had conceded, especially when Carla had said she would pay. Renee always pled poverty; Carla always had more than enough.

Lance picked up on the fifth ring. "Hello."

It was so good to hear his voice. "Hi, Lance … Carla, here."

"Carla! Wow! Good to hear from you. How are things?"

"Not bad … you?"

"Great. I am working on a project—hopefully, have it completed before Christmas." Lance paused. "How are you and Wade doing?"

"He left."

"Sorry."

"Don't be."

"You sound like Mother," Lance accused.

"If I had a little more of Mother in me, I might not have such a problem hanging on to a man." Carla sounded bitter for a moment. "Anyway, I didn't call to discuss my love life. I called about Mother. I thought that maybe this Christmas we could surprise her with a visit; it's been a while."

"Sorry, sis, Tanya surprised me on my birthday with tickets to a resort in the Bahamas. We celebrate with the kids on Christmas Eve; Tanya and I leave on Boxing Day. Why don't you and Renee go?" he suggested.

"We are. I was hoping you'd come too. I have an eerie feeling—like before Dad died. Mother will be 90 in January."

"Tell you what—ring me when you get there, and we can do a conference call," Lance suggested.

"Sure, Lance—you and Tanya work hard; you deserve a holiday. I'll give Mother a hug for you."

"That would be nice. Thanks, sis."

Renee wasn't happy about being coerced into going to Canada for the holidays—especially to see her crusty old mother whom she had never gotten along with. But, Carla was paying, and Renee didn't really have anything better to do. Maybe she'd look up some old school chums while she was in Brantford. She began packing.

"Sophie, I wish you'd come to the Christmas Eve service," Charlie stopped at Sophie's door. "It's Christmas; you shouldn't be alone."

"I'll be alone even if I go. Nobody there of any importance to me," Sophie returned harshly.

"I'll be there," Charlie smiled.

"Your point being?" Sophie limped over to Charlie. "Now, if you don't mind, I'd like to close my door." She returned to the rocker, pulled the blanket around her and closed her eyes. "Why am I so miserable? Probably because not one of them has even called," the words gurgled through the tears in her throat. "May as well sleep––maybe forever!"

The snow was falling in thick sheets. Most flights into the Hamilton Airport had been cancelled. Carla and Renee had been lucky to connect with the last one that had flown in early on Christmas morning. Renee was pouting as she grabbed her suitcase. "We shouldn't have come."

"You won't regret it, Renee. This may be the last Christmas we will have Mother with us. Remember Dad? None of us could make it home the Christmas before he died…"

"Don't guilt me, Carla. Mother will outlive us."

"Why so bitter?"

"Because nothing I ever did pleased her. You and Lance were her favourites."

"Not true. Mother had to be tough—she was harsh on us all. Actually, you got away with a lot more than Lance and I ever did."

Renee snorted and headed to the door. Carla followed and hailed a taxi. What should have been a half hour drive took an hour in the heavy snow. At the hotel, the cab driver unloaded their bags and wished them a Merry Christmas.

"I'll call Lance when we are on our way to mother's so we can arrange a time for the conference call," Carla said. She was puzzled; Lance didn't answer his cellphone.

"Can I help you, sir?"

"Could you tell me if Sophie Baker's daughters are here?"

"Haven't seen anybody come in for Sophie this morning. In fact," the nurse continued; "I haven't even seen Sophie yet. Do you know what room…"

"Lance!" a familiar voice called out. "You are here!"

Lance turned at his sister's voice. "I thought about what you said, Carla. Mother might not be here next Christmas…"

"Who said I wouldn't be here next Christmas?" Sophie's voice entered the foyer. Her cane dropped to the floor as she embraced her three children.

Carla, Renee and Lance each kissed their mother on the cheek and wished her Merry Christmas. Even Renee's eyes were brimming as she embraced the now frail woman who had once been so strong. Sophie's tears ran unashamedly. There were no words that could express her joy on that, her last Christmas morning.

Remember When

Dedicated to Mom and Dad: Alex and Thelma Cushnie

They looked a dashing pair. She sipped from a steaming teacup; he puffed lazily on a timeworn pipe. They sat a proper distance apart on the wicker porch swing, for this seasoned couple would have no gossip spread about them tonight. One could never be sure who was peeking from behind cracked curtains.

It was a choice evening. Stars twinkled brilliantly. Old man moon beamed approvingly. Crickets sang. Soft breezes frolicked with the leaves of an old maple that shaded the miniature white cottage.

"Shame 'bout that little girl gettin' run over t'other day, eh, Ma?" The grey-haired man's voice joined the night sounds.

"Oh yes, a real shame," the elderly woman set her teacup on the wicker table within arm's reach of the swing. "Why I remember when I was a girl, the little boy down the road … oh, what was his name now … Johnny Bellows! That's it! Well, Johnny went and got himself run over by his daddy's truck. Mr. Bellows was getting ready to change the oil and had the truck perched up on blocks. Johnny was playing around and knocked one of the blocks. The truck dropped and began rolling down the drive, running smack over Johnny Bellow's leg. Right lucky he was, not to have broken that leg, I say." The woman took another sip of her tea. "Mind you, all of us children were taught a lesson from Johnny's mistake because our parents used him as an example of what would happen if we played around vehicles propped up on blocks," she added.

"Did you see that article, Emma, 'bout those teenagers vandalizin' the school t'other night?" The man relit his pipe. "Ain't got respect for anyone nowadays—not like us when we was young." Rings of smoke curled lazily around his head.

"Respect? When you were young? Come on now, George; it's me you're talking to now. Oh, I know kids today, some of them anyway, aren't always on the straight and narrow but," Emma began to reminisce, "if I could jog your memory a bit and remind you of the time you and Skylar Morten tied up old Mr. Crabbit's outhouse…"

George slapped his knee and howled. "Do I remember? Boy, do I remember! Skylar and me we roped that outhouse up real good we did. T'wasn't our fault the old geezer was still in it! How was we to know? Guess the old rascal must 'ave fallen asleep, else he would 'ave heard all the noise we made. Must 'ave been a real sound sleeper too, 'cause me and Skylar made noise enough to wake an army barracks!" George chuckled throughout his rendition.

"How ever did Mr. Crabbit get out?" Emma asked. "Didn't you and Skylar make front page news with this little escapade?" she snickered.

George slapped his knee again and his chuckle boomed into a boisterous laugh. "Oh, Emma darlin', I won't ever forget that night. It rained after Skylar and me left; matter o' fact it was spittin' a bit while we was workin'. That rope we tied 'round the outhouse swelled up real big like, it did." George paused to take a puff on his pipe. "Old Mrs. Crabbit must o' started missin' the old man, though for the life of me, can't figure why she would … well, she went lookin' for him and guess where the first place she looked was?" George smiled mysteriously.

"Where, George?" Emma asked knowingly.

"Why down to the old outhouse, that's where! Reckon old Crabbit spent a lot o' his time there," George snickered as he leaned back in the swing.

"I remember when my ma used to tell us girls it was time to clean up the kitchen after supper; I would up myself out of there quicker than a jackrabbit and head straight for the outhouse. I figured I did more than my share of work in the yards for Pa and that I would leave the menial household duties to my two, more feminine sisters. You see, I was looked upon, by Pa, that is, as the son he never had." Emma took a sip of tea.

"Don't you go interruptin' me now, Emma. I'm tryin' to finish this story 'bout old man Crabbit!" George glared at Emma through the pipe's smoke.

"Well, finish it, George! I'm not stopping you!" Emma retorted.

George continued. "Well, Mrs. Crabbit couldn't undo the ropes. She was a nice old soul; used to give Skylar and me cookies all the time. Never had kids o' her own, you know. Anyhow, she had to fetch some help to get the rope undone, and the closest neighbour 'round just happened to be my pa. By this time ol' Crabbit had woke up and was a hollerin' away at the top o' his lungs. Well, my dad didn't 'ave his big clippers, he'd lent 'em out to someone— probably old Crabbit 'cause he was always borrowin' things from Pa ... anyways, Pa took a little hacksaw over to cut through the rope." George paused a moment for breath. "Me and Skylar, we tied it with a big one, we did!

"Well, me and Skylar, we might o' been the ones that tied that door shut, but my pa, he's the one who done the real damage, far as I'm concerned. He pushed so hard against the outhouse while tryin' to cut the rope that the whole thing toppled over! And there stood old Crabbit, scurrying to get his trousers pulled up. Must 'ave been doin' so much hollerin' 'bout bein' locked in that he plumb forgot his pants was down!

"Skylar and me, we sure got a good walloping over that one—we sure did!" George smirked and settled back in the swing for another puff on his pipe. "Was worth it, though!" he added.

"Well George, I wouldn't say what you and Skylar did to old Crabbit was too respectful, would you?" Emma wasn't going to let her original point go astray.

George chose to ignore her impertinence. He peered over the top of his spectacles: "Come to think of it Em, I vaguely remember a time when you wasn't so respectful either. Tried to pull the wool over your ma's eyes, if I recollect. Took a whole week off school while your pa was out of town. Didn't you tell your ma you was sick?" George was trying to take the heat off of him.

"Oh, George! Do you have to conjure up that story?" Emma's face flushed at the horrid memory.

"Yep, come on old woman, tell it all!" George, forgetful of the ever watchful neighbours, reached over and poked Emma gently in the ribs.

She slapped his hand. "Stop it, George! What will the neighbours think?"

"Truthfully, Emma darlin', I don't give a hoot what they think! We bin married fifty years and ain't no one gonna tell me I can't tickle my wife, on my porch, under the light of a full moon. Besides, how do you know we're bein' watched?"

"I just know," Emma stated emphatically. "That old biddy, you know the one, Miss Driddle, who lives two houses down, why she's always nosing out her window.

And, I might add, she has been known to spread some awful gossip about people, and…"

"Emma darlin', quit stallin' and get back to your week off school."

"George, you know the story," Emma looked pleadingly at her husband.

"Get on with it, woman," he said. "Humour me!"

Emma drew in a deep breath. "Well, it all started with this gruesome science project. There was no way on God's green earth that I was going to dissect a frog, let alone a snake! We were expected to do both!" Emma hesitated. "Do you remember Ronnie Pulvert, George?"

"Yeah, what about him?" George's tone indicated a lack of use for the fellow.

"Well, Ronnie was teasing me on the Friday, saying all sorts of awful things about what we would find inside the snakes and frogs when we began dissection on Monday morning. I had nightmares the entire weekend! When Monday morning rolled around, I truly did look dreadful, so when I told Ma I was terribly ill, she believed me. My ma was a gentle soul, bless her heart, and she hated to see anyone suffer, least of all one of her own daughters.

"I decided with Pa gone away for the week on some farm convention thing that I would be able to take the entire week off. He wasn't due back till late Thursday evening. I figured by then most of the dissecting would be finished.

"Well, did things backfire on me! Pa arrived home Thursday all right—Thursday noon! He discovered me, lying on the sitting room couch, absorbed in a good book. I knew all was lost. One might pull the wool over Ma's eyes, but Pa was a different character altogether!

"Pa asked what was wrong with me, and shouldn't I be in school. I pleaded with him that I was truly ill. He cleared his throat, felt my forehead, stated there was not a thing wrong with me and ordered me to school before he throttled me on the spot. I would receive my just desserts, for any deception I had done after supper!" Emma poured herself another tea. "Would you like a cup, George?"

"No thanks, Em. I just want to hear what happened with your science project," he stated smugly.

"I got a D, of course. Oh, the teacher was so nice when I got to school and very willing to give me extra time to complete my project, due to my illness and all; but, I just couldn't do it, George. I burst into tears, ran from the room and confessed all to the headmaster, Mr. Bruins. I was such an excellent student, you know; even he was willing to overlook my indiscretion and grant me the time needed to complete the dissection. I refused! After all, I had principles—principles that included not dissecting innocent creatures!" Emma finished with an adamant nod.

"'Specially snakes and frogs, eh, Em?" laughed George. "What'd yer pa do to you, Em?"

"Pa presented me with a whipping like I'd never had before. It wasn't the not doing of the science project that had upset him; it was the lying to Ma. Pa said I should have told the truth in the beginning." Emma paused. "Guess I should have. That way, my only punishment would have been a D in science!"

Emma settled back in the swing. She cuddled closer to George, sighed, and laid her head on his shoulder. The nosy neighbour was totally forgotten. George was still such a strong man, and handsome too, for all his 83 years.

George slipped his arm around his wife's shoulders and pulled her closer. She was still a stunning woman despite the hard years they had witnessed together. Emma had been his rock, standing staunchly by his side through thick and thin. He couldn't even begin to imagine life without her constant and reassuring presence.

"Remember, Emma darlin', when we was supposed to go ridin' and ol' Duggie took sick? You suggested we both ride Patricia. She was a big, strong mare, she was; a beautiful dapple colour. Shame yer pa had to harness her for farm work." George rambled, bringing up an event they had shared together while they were courting.

"Well, if truth be known, George, I never really believed that story you told about Duggie coming down sick. I always felt you made that up just so we could ride double on Patricia." Emma tried to look stern.

"But you didn't mind a minute did you, Em, ridin' up behind me, with your arms circlin' 'round my waist, all cozy-like?" There was a sly look in old George's eyes.

Emma giggled. "Of course not, George; I didn't mind a bit. But, it was what happened during the ride that I am still not sure of!"

"Do you think yer pa ever believed us?" George queried.

"Not for a moment—not the story you told him. Put yourself in Pa's shoes, George; would you have believed that story had it been your daughter straggling in with her boyfriend an hour after the horse had arrived back to the barn?"

"Reckon I might 'ave found it a pinch unbelievable—but we was tellin' the truth, Emma! I ain't ever had a guilty conscience over that story!" George assured Emma.

"Well, George, at times I've wondered about the stunt Patricia pulled that day. She never acted like that when I rode her alone," Emma stated.

"Emma!" shouted George, totally dismayed. "How could you say such a thing to me after all these years? You were there! You know how quickly she turned and headed into the fruit trees. She decided, of her own accord, to take the shortcut back to the barn. I had no choice but to pull you off with me! We would have been scratched to pieces by all them branches!" George feigned a truly hurt look.

"Well, George, I could never help wondering if Patricia's sudden turn towards the fruit trees hadn't been helped along by a certain someone perched in front of me. And maybe that certain someone preferred to walk me home through the orchard and that having to jump off a runaway horse was an excuse no father could dispute!" Emma laughed lightly. "But, I guess the truth is still hidden inside that certain someone—isn't it, George?"

George let out a howl. "I reckon it is, Emma darlin'— reckon it is."

"Pa will never know now."

"Nope."

"Probably I'll never know either?"

"Probably not."

"That certain someone's secret?"

"Yep."

The grand old pair continued to rock slowly in the wicker swing. The crickets had ceased their songs and retired to bed. The stars still twinkled brightly. Old man moon still smiled down on Emma and George. The breeze had gone elsewhere to play. Miss Driddle's window was unlit. Night slept. The striking, aged couple were serene. Their eyes smiled at each other as they got up and ambled, hand in hand, into their home.

"Been a lovely evening, hasn't it, George?"

"Yep, Emma darlin'; it sure has. A good night for rememberin' … remember when…"

"Oh, George!"

The Graveyard

Dedicated to my adventurous Dad, Alexander Cushnie

Flossie was sending her two oldest sons for some bread. She seldom bought store bread, but she had been feeling poorly of late and had not baked enough to make sandwiches for the children's lunches. She felt guilty for sending them out on such a gloomy night, and it was Devil's Night, when the not so nice neighbourhood kids did horrendous deeds. But Flossie knew that her Alex and George were not of that persuasion.

Flossie handed George some change. "Give my regards to Mr. Blooming." The boys headed for the door. "Better put a jacket on; it looks like quite a wind out there. I don't want you catching a cold and passing it on to the young ones!"

George and Alex grinned at each other before grabbing their jackets. They raced out the door and down the sidewalk, stopping by the big oak tree out in front of the Widow Eliza's house.

"Want to look in her window and see what she's up to?" George snickered.

"Nah. I'd rather we go over to the Oliver place and look in Amy's window," Alex replied.

"Alex has the hots for Amy!" George chanted.

"Do not!"

"Do too!"

The boys began wrestling, falling into the pile of leaves on Widow Eliza's front lawn. The porch light flickered on, and they skedaddled off before she could see who it was.

"Good evening, Mr. Blooming," Alex greeted upon entering the store.

"Evening boys," Mr. Blooming had a friendly voice. "How's your mother doing? Widow Eliza told me she was feeling poorly."

"She has been a tad tired lately," George informed. "She sends her regards to you, though."

"We need a loaf of bread," Alex said, picking what he thought was the largest loaf on the shelf.

George handed Mr. Blooming the money. "See you later, boys; tell your mother I hope she is feeling better soon."

"Sure will," the boys hollered back.

"Wanna take the shortcut, Alex?"

"Through the graveyard?"

"Yeah. I saw them digging when I was on my way home from school. Should we check it out?" George smiled mischievously.

"Sure." Alex followed his brother across the street to the cemetery.

The boys meandered around the gravestones. They stopped and read the inscriptions, laughing at some of the funny names and joking about how lucky they were to have such fine, normal ones. Finally, they came to the freshly dug hole.

"Guess there'll be a funeral tomorrow," George said.

Alex looked thoughtfully at the hole. "I wonder what it would be like to lie down there; sort of get the feel for what it might be like one day when we get dropped in one of these holes."

"I don't think we better," George started to turn away. "Chicken."

"Am not!"

"Are too!"

The boys jumped simultaneously into the hole and lay down side by side. The wind had picked up considerably and leaves were dropping on top of them. They were awed by the brightness of the stars and the fullness of the moon.

"Peaceful here," George commented.

"Yeah, but I think we better get going. Mother will be worried," Alex said.

"Shush!" George whispered. "Do you hear that?"

Alex listened. A tapping sound was coming closer and closer to the hole. "What are we going to do?" he whispered back.

"On the count of three, let's jump out of here and head for home!" George replied shakily. "One ... two ... three!" The boys leapt from the hole and raced home, propelled on by the shrill scream that echoed through the graveyard on their departure. The loaf of bread lay on the ground beside the open grave.

Once inside the back door, they realized they were short a loaf of bread. "What are we going to do?" asked George.

"Must have left it at the grave," Alex commented.

A tapping sound echoed in their ears. It was getting closer. The boy's faces turned ashen. It had followed them home! There was a loud knock. They slipped into the hall closet just before their mother came through to answer the door.

"Well, hello, Eliza."

"Evening, Flossie. Thought I would just drop your bread off; the boys left it in the graveyard. Something must have scared them pretty bad because they took off like a shot. Frightened me near to death when they jumped out of that grave! I just walked over there to visit my Ethan; been a year since his passing." She paused. "I'd appreciate it if the boys could come over tomorrow to rake my leaves; somehow they got scattered—must have been the wind."

"I'll see they do," Flossie smiled. "How's that ankle of yours?"

"Better, should only need the cane for another week."

"Take care now," Flossie shut the door and turned to the slightly open closet. "Boys!"

Deception

Billy was going to have a wonderful day. He got out of bed and stretched his muscles. School started on Tuesday, and he had planned something extra special for his Saturday. He smiled all the way down the stairs, but when he arrived in the kitchen, he saw his mom at the table writing on a piece of paper. Somehow he got a spooky feeling his plans might be thwarted, and his spirits fell.

"Good morning, Billy. This is a list of chores for you to do today," his mom looked up with a smile.

"But Kenny and I were going fishing!" Billy protested.

"Not until the chores are done."

"But the best fish are early in the morning!"

"Not today, Billy. Now, let me go over this list with you."

Billy's spirit fell even further as his mom read off his jobs for the day: "Sweep and vacuum the floors, empty the garbage and make sure the big pails are out for the 1:00 pick-up, clean your room and do your laundry!" Billy knew he could get through the floors and the garbage in no time, but his room was another matter! "I am going shopping and then out for lunch with your grandma, Billy. When you get your work done, you may call Kenny and go fishing. Just leave me a note on the kitchen table, so I know where you are."

Billy watched his mom's car leave. He went into the living room, plunked himself on the couch and turned on the T.V. He needed to think things out and figure a way to go fishing like he had planned, and still get his chores done! The phone rang.

"Hello." Billy's voice was despondent.

"Hey Billy, are you ready yet? I got the fishin' poles and the bait. Do you have lunch packed?" Kenny's excited voice came over the line.

"I have a problem; my mom left me a list of things to do before I can go out anywhere."

"But we've had this planned for an entire week!" Kenny shouted into the phone. There was a pause on the line and then, "I've got an idea..."

Billy listened and as Kenny finished talking, Billy's glum face turned into a beam of sunshine. "You're a genius, Kenny! I think that will work! And my mom will never know. She won't be back for hours anyway because grandma is a pretty slow shopper and always gets my mom to do extra things for her!"

Billy hung up the phone and got busy making some peanut butter and jam sandwiches. He made a bit of a mess on the counter and the knife fell out of the jam jar and onto the floor. "I can clean that later," Billy grinned as he moved on to his next task. He looked in the fridge and grabbed a couple of apples from the crisper and some juice boxes from the top shelf. As he was reaching for them, he knocked over the milk jug. "I can clean that up later, too," he reasoned as he shut the fridge door on the mess. Billy put all the goodies into his backpack and headed out the door to meet Kenny. The two boys met up at Waterwork's Park and then took one of the off-beat trails to get down to the river. They had scoped out the perfect fishing spot earlier in the summer.

Billy's mom was having a delightful time shopping with her mother—until her mother had a slight dizzy spell.

"Oh dear, I am not feeling too well; I think we should just skip lunch today," she said as she looked for a place to sit down.

"Maybe if you just sit for a few minutes, Mom, and have a drink of water, you will feel better."

"No dear, I would like you to take me home; I'd like to lie down."

Billy's mom opened the back door and stepped into the kitchen. "Billy, I'm home."

Silence greeted her. She dropped her purse on the table and looked around. The counter was a mess. The peanut butter and jam jars were sitting open beside a loaf of bread. She gazed down to the floor and saw the sticky knife. She walked over to the fridge and opened it to get a bottle of water.

"What the ... BILLY!"

More silence.

"Billy," she called as she headed upstairs to his room.

More silence.

She opened his bedroom door. The mess was still there, but there was no Billy. Her face turned red: "That boy had better not be out fishing!" she mumbled angrily as she shut his door.

Billy and Kenny were having a grand time on the riverbank. They had yet to catch a fish but it was sure fun hooking the worms on their lines and casting them into the water. Kenny's line had tugged at one point but it had turned out to be an old running shoe. There had been a few nibbles from experienced fish too, because a couple of times when they had pulled their lines in, the worms had been half-eaten.

Midmorning, the boys polished off their apples, and by the time the sun reached her peak, they were digging into the peanut butter and jam sandwiches. Wrestling had always been a ritual of their time together and it was no exception on this fishing day. The fish weren't biting anyway. Kenny instigated the onslaught by throwing his empty drink box at Billy. Billy wasn't impressed at getting hit in the back of the head.

"Ouch!" he laughed as he leaped over a small rock and then tackled his pal.

The two friends grappled until they were both out of breath. "Enough!" they cried at the same time.

Billy stood. His head was spinning. As he walked back to his fishing pole, he lost his balance and tumbled down to the water's edge. When he didn't come up the bank right away, Kenny hollered out, "You okay bro?"

No answer.

Kenny felt a moment of panic. He got up to take a look. Billy lay still on the river's shore; there was a red pool beside his head.

Billy's mom was so angry that Billy had disobeyed her, but at the same time, she was worried because he hadn't left a note and she wasn't sure exactly where he was. The Grand River was pretty big, and he had a lot of favourite spots where he and Kenny liked to go. She had figured out who he was with after having called Kenny's mom who had confirmed the boys were out fishing.

"Is there a problem?" Kenny's mom had asked.

"Not for Kenny!"

Just as Billy's mom was getting ready to call his dad, the phone rang. She snatched it up. "Is this Mrs. Morton?"

"Yes."

"This is the Brantford General Emergency Department. Please don't worry now; we don't want to alarm you … your son is fine … just a little gash on the side of his head … it will only take about ten stitches to close it up … the doctor is with him now … we need you to come and pick him up though…"

Billy's mom dropped the phone and raced out the door.

"How bad is it?" Kenny asked. "Pretty bad," Billy replied.

Kenny had been allowed to visit his friend but Billy's mom had told him it would only be for about ten minutes. Her eyebrows had crunched together as she had told him she didn't think they could concoct any grand schemes in that short space of time.

"Yer mom's furious, isn't she?"

"Yep." Billy looked away. "I've been grounded for a whole month."

"A month!"

"It gets worse."

"How could it? A month is, like, forever!"

"She has me doing chores every night and all day on Saturday. When there is nothin' here for me to do, I will be going over to my grandma's house to do chores there. Mom says that grandma's yard needs a good cleaning and I am just the person to do it!"

"How can she make you do all that?" Kenny exclaimed. "You're wounded!"

Billy sighed. "Apparently not seriously enough to prevent me from starting out with light duty." He paused. "Look at the bright side, Kenny; October is still a pretty good month for fishin' and we usually have Indian Summer around then."

"Maybe I can help with your chores. After all, it was my idea that got you in trouble."

"Thanks but no thanks. I made the decision. I should have known better; it was the chance I took and it is a lesson learned."

"Yeah ... well, I better get going. Your mom said I could only stay for ten minutes." Kenny paused. "Besides, I have a few of my own chores to do; Mom wasn't too happy about me convincing you to go fishing before your work was done!" he confessed.

The two boys walked over to Billy's window. They knew the river was just beyond the trees. They could hear it beckoning to them. They imagined the fish leaping about. They turned around and Billy walked his friend downstairs to the front door. They gave their customary special handshake.

"Billy!" The tone of the voice from the kitchen indicated that his month of hard labour was about to begin!

The Birth Certificate

Dedicated to Patricia … I mean, Teresa

Teresa hadn't been on a holiday since her honeymoon 19 years ago, and that had been a short two days at Niagara Falls. Her husband, George, had come home from work a week ago and surprised her with two airline tickets to Scotland. Teresa blushed as she remembered that moment.

"Next month is our 20th Anniversary, and I thought it was time we got away," George had smiled his boyish smile—it was one of the things she had fallen in love with on their first meeting.

"I don't know if I can get the time off work, George."

"I already looked after that; I spoke to your boss, and she thought it was a great idea for you to get away."

"I see." Teresa had not known George had it in him to plan something so big. "How long have you been scheming this?"

"A couple months."

"Who else knew about it?"

"Everyone."

"And no one told me?"

"They weren't supposed to, Teresa—it was to be a surprise!" George had smirked.

Teresa had thought a moment. She needed an excuse to get out of this, for even as much as she felt the idea was delightful, there was just so much to do and she was not sure she could manage to get ready so quickly. "Who will look after Bob?" Bob was a cat. Their son, Jesse, had left him behind when he got married.

"Your sister, Linda."

"What about the house? We've never left it for so long before!"

George had reached across the empty space between them and drawn Teresa into his arms. She remembered how his bright blue eyes had gazed down into her dark chocolate ones as he said: "It's no use, woman; it's all looked after. We leave in two months; we just need to get our passports and pack!"

"I'll need to get my birth certificate first," Teresa had mentioned.

"Well, get on it then, woman!"

Teresa took a sip of coffee. Every morning, George left a Timmy's coffee on the table for her before he headed off to work. She decided to call her sister Shirley to ask her to get the birth certificate and passport application forms off the computer for her.

"I've already run them off," Shirley said.

"Oh, right—you were in on this too."

Shirley laughed. "I'll bring them over this morning."

After filling out the forms, they drove to Hamilton to make the application in person. There was no time to waste because Teresa knew she couldn't apply for the passport until she had her birth certificate. She paid the extra fee to have it expedited and then went home to start packing. There was so much to do!

A week and a half passed and still, there was no sign of a birth certificate. The woman at the government office had said she should receive it within ten days. Teresa began to worry. Should she call and see what the holdup was? She took a sip of her Timmy's and then started flipping through the phonebook. Her phone rang.

"Who could that be," she mumbled. "Hello."

"Hello, is this Teresa Dolhen?"

"Yes."

"I'm calling in regards to your birth certificate application; there seems to be a problem with your name…"

"My name?" Teresa interrupted.

"Yes, it appears you are not who you think you are."

"Oh, I know who I am!" Teresa was wondering if her son was playing a trick on her.

"Well, it appears that whoever filled out your birth registration form, put your name down as Patricia, not Teresa; do you know anything about this?"

Teresa was flabbergasted! There was only one way this could possibly have happened. "I'll get back to you," she garbled as she hung up the phone. Then she dialled Shirley's number. "Shirley, you'll never guess what grandpa did!"

"What?"

"Remember how he always used to call me Patricia?"

"Yes."

"And when I would try and correct him and say my name was Teresa?"

"Yes."

"And we just thought it was his French accent?"

"Yes."

"Remember Mom saying that grandpa had registered my birth at the city hall?"

"Yes," Shirley sighed; "get to the point, Teresa!"

"Well, he registered me as Patricia, and now I can't get my birth certificate, and if I can't get that, I can't get my passport, and I won't be able to go to Scotland with George, and…"

"Whoa, Teresa; I have tomorrow off so we'll go to Hamilton and get this all straightened out."

George put his arm around Teresa. It wouldn't be long before they landed. The Highlands of Scotland were beckoning from the plane windows. "Okay, woman of mine—Patricia!" he smirked.

"That's not funny, it almost ruined our trip!"

"It worked out, didn't it?

"I guess."

"We're here now, aren't we?"

"Yes."

"Patricia…"

"George!"

Never Again

Never again would anyone refer to Mary Nelson as a misfit. It had been ten years since she left the town she grew up in and Mary had worked hard to create her new image.

She stopped her little sports car in front of Diggers Water Hole—still, the only tavern in town—took a deep breath as she got out of the car, then walked into where she knew most of the old gang would be hanging out on a Saturday night. The reaction was as she expected from this lot—catcalls, whistles and shouts of, "Hey baby, come sit over here," as they patted their laps.

Mary smiled amiably to everyone as she made her way to the bar and took a seat on a high stool. She crossed her legs and the slit of her skirt exposed the long, lean limbs.

Slowly, she turned and faced the bartender, "White spritzer," she smiled, recognizing Bobby Jo Barnes, former captain of the high school football team.

"Hey there, pretty lady, just get into town?" Bobby Jo flashed a smile. He still had the gold tooth. Mary remembered the day he had lost that front tooth. It had been the championship game, and she had been watching from behind the bleachers. No one noticed her there.

In fact, no one had ever really paid much attention to Mary when she was growing up. She had been referred to as the 'poor, white trash kid' whose pappy had left because she had been too ugly to look at. It had been rumoured that even her momma couldn't stand being around Mary and had finally up and left town the day Mary turned sixteen. Little did they know the real truth about her parents—little did any of them care. Mary left too, on her twentieth

Mary M. Cushnie-Mansour

birthday, and had vowed never to return. But things had changed in the past ten years, and she had some unfinished business to tend to here.

Mary smiled sweetly to Bobby Jo as she answered him. "No, actually I have been here before."

"You don't say," Bobby Jo was trying to turn on the charm. "How could I have missed someone like you?" Mary noticed his thickening waistline.

She picked up her drink and threw a five-spot on the bar. "Keep the change, lover." She knew he had always thought of himself in that manner.

She slipped off the stool and meandered around the tables, pretending unawareness of the staring eyes and murmuring voices. When she reached the jukebox, Mary flipped through the charts until she came to the song she was looking for and then slipped a coin into the slot. The music started.

Mary glanced over to a table in the corner and saw the one person from this town she was happy to see. He had been the only kid from her childhood who had ever shown her kindness.

She sauntered over to him. Everyone was gawking. The only distinguishable sound in the bar was the song ... *and down the road, I looked and there walked Mary, hair of gold and lips like cherry...*

Mary flipped her long golden locks and leaned on the young man's table. "Wanna dance—Jacob?" She emphasized his name.

Jacob Michaels looked up in surprise. He hesitated a moment as he stared into the eyes of this beautiful woman in front of him. A flicker of recognition sparkled in his eyes.

Leisurely, he stood up and followed Mary onto the dance floor. Everyone watched as Jacob, otherwise known as the 'town geek,' slow danced with this goddess who had just walked into their bar. Mary laid her head upon his shoulder. Jacob leaned over and whispered something in her ear. She looked up into his eyes and smiled.

The song ended … *It's good to touch the green, green grass of home.*

Jacob gave Mary a hug, thanked her for the dance and walked back to his table. As Mary headed for the door, she noticed several of the old gang racing to Jacob's table. She could tell they were plying him with questions as to who the stranger was.

Jacob just sat there and smiled. He was enjoying the thrill of the game. It was about time these guys were put in their place—he'd endured their teasing and taunting long enough. Mary turned, before going out the door, "See you later, Jacob; ten o'clock at the Four Seasons!"

"I'll be there, Mary."

The incessant questioning ceased. A bleach-blond woman with a cigarette hanging from the corner of her mouth and a rye and coke in her hand, spoke up. "Mary, who?" she slurred.

"Mary Nelson," Jacob smirked as he stood, strolled to the bar, threw some coin for his drink to Bobby Jo, then followed Mary out the door. He checked his watch. Nine forty-five. He had fifteen minutes before he was to meet Mary at the hotel.

"God, life is good," he smiled as he got into his Lincoln and drove to meet his only childhood friend. He pulled up in front of the Four Seasons, reached into the glove-box and retrieved his wedding ring. Mrs. Michaels would be waiting for him inside, and the people in this town had no clue just how perfect life really was for the 'poor white trash kid' and the 'town geek!'

Faceless

Dedicated to all the 'Pretty Women' who have not yet met their 'Prince Charming'

She turned off the movie even though it wasn't finished yet and looked around her small, scantily furnished apartment. Tears choked at the corners of her eyes. It had been years since she'd actually cried. She closed her eyes and tried to dream sweet dreams, but all that seemed to kaleidoscope before her were the same excruciating scenes of her tortured childhood…

Upon first glance, one would have thought that the picture of the young girl on the swing was one of blissful innocence. Her face was tiny; her eyes were an innocent blue. Her cheeks were a rosy red upon a palate of pale skin. She sighed contentedly, and her lips smiled as the swing swung back and forth. Her blond curls bounced in the light breeze.

But the next slide was different—an obscure figure stepped out from behind the tree. It stood there for a moment, silently scrutinizing the child; a sadistic curl to its lips as its tongue flicked in and out, resembling a rattler's warning.

The little girl's innocent blue eyes darkened in a face that had turned ashen. Her breathing became laboured. Perspiration bubbled on her forehead, dripping down into her furrowed eyebrows. The tiny fingers became white at the knuckles as they clenched the rope on the swing. The swing slowed to a standstill as the figure approached. Its hands reached up and covered the little girl's trembling ones. Its lips curled up, revealing a yellow smile.

The walk to the house took forever as the little girl dragged her feet through the grass and then struggled up the steep concrete steps. The back door creaked open. There was another figure standing in a shadowy corner of the kitchen. It was silent. All the little girl saw was its back as she passed through, down the long gloomy hall to her room at the back of the house.

Snap...

The little girl was sitting at the dinner table. Her innocent blue eyes were red-rimmed. Her face was mottled purple. Her hands twisted nervously on her lap as she waited for her food to be served. Two figures were sitting at the table with her—the one with the yellow smile and the one whose face she could not see...

The young woman woke up. She glanced at the clock. It was only 2:00 a.m. She was so tired, yet sleep never seemed to ease her fatigue. She'd given up on trying to figure out what would. She got up from her chair and made a trip to the bathroom, glancing in her bedroom on the way past. She felt dizzy. She'd been getting a lot of dizzy spells lately—maybe she should give the doctor a call and get checked out. She splashed some water on her face and then looked into the mirror.

One would never guess she was only 29. Her blue eyes were dull and lifeless; dark circles surrounded them. Her cheeks were artificially coloured; her skin, sallow. Her blond curls had been replaced with a short, spiky mousey-brown hairdo. Her lips had not been able to smile for years.

She stepped back from the mirror and studied the full effect of time. She was rail thin, having lost another unaffordable ten pounds within the past two weeks. It didn't matter what she did to try and gain weight. "Okay," she remarked to the mirror's reflection. "I'll call the doctor in the morning."

She returned to the living room, flopped down on the couch, and flicked the television back on. She may as well finish the movie even though she knew it off by heart, having watched it over and over and over. She didn't know why she tortured herself so, because each time it ended it felt as though another nail had pierced her coffin...

The morning sun streamed in the window, settling on the young woman's sleeping face. Her hand reached up and brushed away a fly which had landed on her nose. She opened her eyes, stood up and walked down the hall to her bedroom. She glanced around at the emptiness. She straightened the covers on the dishevelled bed she never slept in, and then walked over to the dresser and gathered the bills which were sitting on top of her jewellery box. She counted them; she'd have enough now to pay the rent for another month.

"Not all movies have a fairy tale ending, Julia," she whispered huskily as she put the money in her purse.

In From the Cold

Frederick had lived on the streets for years. This past winter had been particularly demanding, for two reasons. One, there had been an over-abundance of snow, which had made it difficult for him to get around; the other—Tracey.

He had come upon Tracey one cold December night. She had been curled up, sound asleep, in his spot. At first, he was angry and had been ready to give her the boot out, but then, as he stood watching her...

She was wrapped in one of his old tattered blankets. Her face was mottled with bruises; her eyes were swollen and red, lines of agony rippled down her cheeks. Her fingers were blue, nails bitten to the quick. He saw the soles of her feet through the over-worn runners.

Even he had boots, retrieved from a used clothing bin. It was getting more difficult to salvage nowadays because the bins were emptied more often; Frederick did have a friend on the inside who watched out for some of his needs though.

"Maybe I'll drop by today and get the girl some things," Frederick mumbled. He leaned against the wall, reached inside his coat pocket and pulled out a bottle. It was just pop tonight—that was all he'd been able to find in the garbage can. He reached into his other pocket for his cigarette. It was three-quarters smoked—by someone else. He couldn't figure out why someone would have thrown it away, but hey, who was he to question. He let it hang from his mouth, breathing in the taste; he had run out of matches.

Frederick awoke just before noon. The girl was gone. He cursed because his bones felt brittle from the position he'd slept in. However, being a street veteran, he knew she would return to this spot at some point. He headed off to the nearest second hand store.

"Good morning, Frederick," a cheery voice greeted him as he walked past the store door. "Looks like we're in for another big storm."

Frederick gazed at the sky. He shivered at the thought of another storm so soon.

"Want a coffee?"

"Sure, Meg ... got any matches?"

Meg disappeared into the store and returned a couple minutes later with a coffee and a pack of matches. "Thanks ... any new stuff in the bin?" he asked as he lit his cigarette.

"Not sure; I just started my shift. Take a look before Mike gets out there and empties it," Meg smiled.

Frederick rummaged through the bin. He found a pair of winter boots, a coat, a hat and some gloves, and then his eye caught something pink in a black garbage bag. He pulled the bag apart, and it revealed a beautiful quilt. "Well, I'll be," he smiled. "Just what she needs."

He wrapped the treasures in the blanket and headed home. Along the way, he stopped by the french fry wagon; Mildred always gave him a sampling. Sometimes the potatoes were a bit hard and they hurt his gums, but they were free and filled a spot in the pit of his stomach.

When Frederick arrived at his spot, there was no sign of the girl. He set the things down and then wandered off again. In the evening he returned to find her sitting there wrapped in the pink blanket and wearing the clothes.

"Thank you," she whispered when she saw him.

"No problem, girlie ... What's yer name?"

"Tracey."

"Don't you have a home?"

Tracey looked away. Frederick sat down beside her, and they talked deep into the night. The wind picked up; snow pellets began to fall. He listened. She was 16, pregnant, and had been kicked out of her home because of drug use—her parents didn't know she was pregnant. When she had told her 21-year-old boyfriend, he'd gotten angry. They had fought verbally, and then he had started beating on her.

She had nowhere to go; no one to turn to. She had burned a lot of bridges. Frederick mentioned a place where she might go—better than the streets. She smiled and thanked him, then pulled a couple chocolate bars from her pocket. He did not bother to ask how she had gotten them. When Frederick awoke the next morning, Tracey was gone.

Winter became spring, and then, summer. Frederick was rummaging in the garbage when he noticed the newspaper and the birth announcement…

Frederick McCrew, born June 21, 2008, to Tracey. Many thanks to the nurses at the BGH and to a friend, Frederick, who was there for me when I needed a shoulder to lean on.

Frederick grinned as he ripped out the birth announcement. He folded it neatly and placed it in his pocket. There was a lightness to his step as he headed home that had not been there for years.

Pearl

*January 1992—Dedicated to a little girl, Pamela,
who found no real joy in her Christmas gifts*

It was going to be a bleak Christmas. The coal mines had been shut down for six months and there was no hope of them opening any time soon. Generations of Samantha's family had worked in the mines.

Samantha was busy in the kitchen, filling the baskets Mama gave to the less fortunate every Christmas. Mama had baked late into the night to ensure enough for everyone. It baffled her why Mama continued the tradition this year when they were barely scraping by. But that was Mama, always thinking of others, and Samantha knew she would insist on delivering the baskets tonight, on the traditional eve of Christmas Eve. And, as always, she would help.

Samantha's mama was not well. She had caught a virus back in October and had never fully recovered. "Samantha," a frail woman entered the cottage. "Are the baskets ready, dear? I see a storm brewing; we shall need speedy feet if we are to beat it home."

"Mama, you look so tired; couldn't we deliver these tomorrow?"

"I'm afraid not, love; they must go out tonight," Mama sighed wearily.

They loaded the baskets into the push-wagon used to get vegetables from town on market days and then set off. The wind gained velocity as mother and daughter walked through the village. Soon the only warmth they found was the hugs received from thankful recipients.

Samantha gazed up at the sky. It was blacker than ever. She glanced at her mama whose step had become a tired shuffle. She checked the wagon—two baskets left.

"Mama," Samantha reached over and shook her mama's shoulder. The wind was vicious now. Pellets of ice bit into any exposed skin. "Mama, you head home; I'll finish up. Just tell me who these are for."

Samantha was surprised when Mama nodded, a sure sign she was not well. "One for Mrs. Hodge; the other for old widow Edna."

Samantha's breath caught sharply in her throat. Old Edna! The witch! That was what the children in the village called her. Samantha hoped mama hadn't noticed her worry.

Samantha arrived at Mrs. Hodge's door. She had buried three husbands; all had met their deaths in the mines. She always swore she would never marry again, but Samantha wondered who would be Mrs. Hodge's next victim!

"Oh, bless your mama, child," Mrs. Hodge said, taking the basket. "There's no one like her. She takes such good care of the likes of us," she added tearfully. "You look after her; she didn't look too well last time I saw her. Make her up some chicken broth; that will help her, it will."

"Thanks for the advice, Mrs. Hodge; I'll be sure to do that. I must be on my way though, I've one more basket to deliver."

"Where to, love?" Mrs. Hodge inquired nosily.

"Old widow Edna's."

Mrs. Hodge gasped. "You take care now, Samantha; wish the family a Merry Christmas. Big storm coming in, you'd better hurry." The door shut quickly, leaving Samantha alone in the flying snowflakes.

Old widow Edna lived down by the closed coal mine. Rumours said it was really because of her that the mine had been shut down. She had caught her husband cheating with a young local girl. Edna had cursed and shrieked upon finding the two intertwined, and had chased them from her cottage with a large butcher knife. They had headed into the old mine and the main shaft had collapsed. The two were never seen again.

A week later, the mine had been labelled unsafe, and the entrance was sealed shut. Edna had stayed in the cottage. Some of the town's people said she was still waiting for him to return, because, despite his wayward ways, Edna had truly loved him.

The snow was so thick now that Samantha could not see two feet in front of her. She tripped over a rock and fell to the ground. Picking herself up, she brushed the snow off and pushed on. Finally, a beckoning light beamed to her from the window of Edna's cottage. Samantha stomped up to the door and knocked loudly. It seemed like ages before the door creaked open.

"What you doin' girl, out on a night like this? You'll catch yer death." Edna squinted. "Who is you anyways?"

"I'm Pearl Henry's daughter, Samantha, and I have your Christmas basket," Samantha answered.

Edna's face softened at the mention of Pearl's name. Pearl was the only person in town who did not torture her with obscenities or lies. Pearl was indeed one of God's angels; always showing up with something just as the cupboard was getting bare. Oh yes, Edna knew Pearl well.

"Well, here is your basket, Edna; I should be getting along before the storm gets any worse."

"Wait, I have something for Pearl." Edna disappeared inside. She returned with a big bag of coal. "There, that ought to keep yer mama warm over Christmas," she said, hoisting it onto the cart.

"But..." Samantha protested.

"No buts, girl! This is my way." She scrutinized Samantha. "Yer a lot like her; I kin tell. Jus' wait another moment."

Edna returned, this time with a small black bag. "Here, this is for you. Treasure its contents and always remember this: old, dirty and ugly something may be on the outside, but inside, that's where you'll find the real goodness and beauty. You are so like Pearl ... treasure her ... treasure my gift," she muttered. "Merry Christmas," she added as the door closed. Samantha opened the pouch and peeked inside. What in the world! A piece of coal! What was crazy old Edna thinking?

When Samantha arrived home, she found her mama, wrapped in blankets, sitting by the coal stove. "Papa, is Mama okay?" she asked, noticing the worried look on her father's face.

"No, Samantha darlin', she's not. Yer mama's burnin' a high fever. I've sent yer brother, David, fer the doc, but on a night like this, who knows if either o' them will git through."

Samantha swallowed her tears. She watched her mama's shoulders shake with silent coughing. Why did mama always try to be so brave? Why didn't she just acknowledge the pain? Oh, Mama! You have never harmed anyone! Everyone loves you. Why is God taking you from me, Mama?

Anger smothered Samantha's pain. Where was her brother with the doctor? The storm was banging furiously at the cottage walls. Maybe David had fallen and was lying unconscious under a mound of freezing snow. Maybe he had not even reached Dr. Moyer's.

"Samantha, could you fetch some more coal; the stove's dyin'. If'n we run out a'fore Christmas, yer brothers and me kin go diggin' fer more."

"We got plenty of coal, Papa," Samantha informed. "Old widow Edna gave us a big bag in return for the food Mama sent."

Samantha left to fetch the coal. She had not realized how heavy the bag really was until she tried lifting it from the wagon. She wondered how old Edna had even carried it. She also pondered about the little sack still nestled in her pocket, but that could wait.

"David! Dr. Moyer!" Samantha thought to call out before going back into the cottage. "David! Dr. Moyer!" No use; the wind just kept shoving the names back into her mouth.

Papa took the bag of coal from Samantha's arms and put some into the stove. Samantha removed her winter coat and hung it by the door. She took the little black sack from her coat pocket, then went and sat down beside her mama. "Look what old widow Edna gave me, Mama." Samantha held the bag up. "Just a piece of coal inside. She mentioned something about not looking so much at how things look on the outside; we need to look inside for the goodness and beauty. What could a piece of coal have to do with that? Do you understand what she meant, Mama?"

Pearl tried to look inside the sack, but another fit of coughing racked her body. "Later ... my love..." she managed between coughs. "Later."

Samantha slipped the sack into her apron pocket and headed for the kitchen to prepare something for her mama. She found a pot of stew left over from lunch, drained off some broth and set it on the stove. Hopefully, it would ease mama's cough and warm her bones.

"Come, Pearl. You must git into bed. You'll be much warmer there." John Henry tried drawing his wife from the chair.

She motioned him off. "No, John ... must wait ... for the ... doctor." Another coughing fit consumed her.

"Sam darlin', give me a hand 'ere with yer mama. See if you kin convince her to git into bed; she'll listen to you," Papa pleaded.

"Come on, Mama," Samantha lifted her mama gently by the elbow. "You should be in bed. Dr. Moyer would want you to be resting."

Pearl gazed lovingly at Samantha, a daughter anyone would envy having. She was Pearl's rock. She allowed herself to be led by her child. Samantha propped the pillows behind her mama. She pulled the down quilt up, nestling it close to the heaving chest. "Relax, Mama; I'll fetch your broth."

The anxious ticking of the clock pushed time forward. Samantha spooned the broth into her mama's mouth, and when it was finished, Pearl closed her eyes and fell into a restless slumber. Beads of perspiration spotted her face and trickled down onto the collar of her nightgown.

"Yer mama's sicker'n I've ever seen her, Samantha. What are we gonna do?"

"We are going to look after her, Papa; Mama is going to get better, for good this time," Samantha answered.

Samantha's father shuffled wearily over to his chair. Tears crowded the corners of his eyes. "We both better rest while yer mama sleeps," he mumbled. It wasn't long before he was snoring.

Samantha wanted to stay awake in case David and Dr. Moyer arrived. She tidied the kitchen, constantly watching the clock. Where were they? David had been gone far too long. Had God forsaken them too?

Her stomach growled, reminding her she had not eaten supper yet. She scooped some stew into a bowl and glanced at the time again. Seven o'clock. Surely something had happened. Or, were they just taking the longer, safer route, staying close to the houses, to be guided by the village lights and have some shelter from the vicious winds.

Samantha was halfway through her bowl of stew when she heard the stamping feet. "At last," she breathed. "Papa! Papa! They're here!" Samantha shook his shoulder on the way to the door. However, before she reached it, the door flew open, revealing David and Dr. Moyer. They resembled frosty snowmen.

"Come, warm yourselves by the stove," Samantha ordered. "I'll get you a bowl of stew and make some tea."

"Lovely, dear, just lovely." Dr. Moyer's frozen face cracked into a humungous smile. "Spot of spirits in the tea might be in good order as well. Did your mama make that stew?" Samantha nodded.

"Your mama makes the best stew I've ever tasted, but that is something you must promise you won't ever tell Mrs. Moyer!"

Samantha laughed. Dr. Moyer was such a jolly man. He had been the town doctor forever. Lately, however, she had noticed deep lines around his eyes, extensive greying, and sagging shoulders. Time and hard work were taking their toll.

His bowl empty, Dr. Moyer stood up. "I'll look to Pearl now."

Pearl must have felt his presence. Her eyes fluttered open, and she smiled. "So good to see you, Dr. Moyer."

He took her hands in his: "How are you feeling, Pearl darling?" A worried look shadowed his face as he gazed into her eyes. He didn't like what he saw. Dr. Moyer took out his stethoscope and listened to Pearl's chest. His frown deepened. "John," he called; "a word with you, please." The men walked to the far side of the room. Dr. Moyer spoke in a hushed voice and kept shaking his head. Samantha and David looked at each other.

"Oh God," David sobbed, "why our mama?"

Samantha embraced her brother. "It's okay, David, don't worry ... Mama will get better; I know she will."

David pulled away. "Don't fool yourself, Sam! Look at Dr. Moyer's face—the way he's shaking his head— Mama isn't going to get better. She's going to die, and that just isn't fair!" David turned and ran up the stairs to the loft where he slept.

Dr. Moyer and John returned to Pearl's bedside. The doctor handed John a bottle of medicine. "Give her a spoonful whenever needed, John, and keep her as comfortable as possible. That's all we can do for her now." He snapped his bag shut. Turning, he saw Samantha's look of despair and realized the child must already know. "How lucky John is to have a child so much like the wife he is about to lose," the doctor thought to himself.

"You must stay the night," John suggested. "The storm is far too fierce to go back out there. Besides, Mrs.

Moyer knows where you are if anyone else should need you."

Dr. Moyer nodded. He knew it would be foolish to attempt this weather again tonight. John fetched some bedding. "Couch, okay?"

"That'll be fine; thank you, John. Pearl should sleep a few hours with that sedative I gave her. You better get some rest as well." Turning to Samantha, he added: "You too, love; get some sleep." Dr. Moyer nestled himself under the cover and was snoring within seconds.

Too exhausted to work any longer, Samantha just set the dishes in the sink. She wiped her hands on her apron, and her fingers bumped against the piece of coal. As Samantha drew out the bag Edna had given her, it slipped from her hand and fell to the floor. "What in the world?" she exclaimed peering inside.

The piece of coal had crumbled. Samantha noticed something small, white and round buried in the rubble. She dumped the contents onto the counter and picked up the white object. Holding it up to the light, Samantha caught her breath. "A pearl! How in the world did this beautiful pearl get inside a piece of black coal?" The living room clock chimed twelve times. Samantha turned off the light and went to bed. She would worry in the morning about why a pearl was inside a piece of coal.

Dreams flooded Samantha's sleep. Hideous, skeletal figurations flitted around in a boarded-up coal mine. Two of the skeletons floated close to each other and joined their bony fingers. Suddenly, rearing up behind them was old widow Edna, her face contorted with rage. In her right hand was an enormous butcher knife. But the blade was directed at Samantha. Edna was laughing—a hideous sound, rippled with evil and insanity. Just as the knife was about to plunge into Samantha's chest, it became a small, black sack. Widow Edna's face softened, breaking into smiles, radiating love.

"Look to the inside of things, deary. Old, dirty, and ugly something may be on the outside; but inside, that's where you'll find the real goodness and beauty. You are deserving of this gift I give you. You are so like her, Pearl, ... such a precious jewel ... treasure the contents..."

Samantha awoke with an unsettled feeling. The sun was just beginning to stretch her arms to embrace the day. Samantha crept quietly to her door, opened it, and peered over to her mama's bed. She froze. There beside her mama, was the hunched over, quietly sobbing figure of her father. Samantha shut her door.

Anger ripped through her. Tears flooded her eyes. Through their mist, she noticed the pearl on her night table. She grabbed it and threw it at the wall. "Beauty! Goodness! Where did it get you, Mama? An early grave?"

When the pearl hit the wall, the room filled with such an intense light that Samantha was forced to cover her eyes. Finally, she dared to look up. She squinted and rubbed her eyes. Before her stood an angel that could have been her mama's identical twin.

"Samantha," the voice was soothingly familiar. "Please, my child, don't weep for me. I'm okay now ... the pain is gone."

"But, Mama, how can this be? How can you be?" Samantha was confused. "Are you ... are you..." Samantha couldn't say the word.

"Yes, dear, I am, yet I am not. Edna foresaw what was going to happen to me. Somehow, she fixed it so we could be together whenever you needed me. I don't know how my spirit lives on in the pearl, but it is Edna's gift to both of us—to ease the pain of our parting."

The angel floated closer and put her arms around Samantha. Warmth flooded into her body. She nestled her head on her mama's shoulder and wept. "Whenever you need me, dear, just take the pearl, throw it to the floor and I will appear. This gift is ours for as long as you feel the need for it."

"Will anyone else be able to see you, Mama?"

"No." Pearl held Samantha's face in her hands. "Now, what you must do is go out there and look after them. Your father will be lost without me; your brothers, especially David, will be devastated. Tell everyone I am okay; I am happy. Tell them I will be watching over them as I have always done. Tell them to celebrate Christmas as it is meant to be. Tell them that is how Pearl would want it. Tell them everything will be okay." The angel gave Samantha a gentle push towards the door. To her surprise, it opened automatically.

Samantha went to her father and put her arms around him. His face was contorted with pain. She saw Dr. Moyer's face etched with sorrow. David sat in a shadowy corner, rocking back and forth in silent anguish.

"Come, Papa. Let Dr. Moyer handle things now. Come sit in the kitchen; I'll brew you some tea."

John Henry looked up at his daughter's radiant face. "How could she not be grieving?" he pondered. "Her mother is gone ... gone forever!"

"Everything will be fine, Papa; you'll see. Mama wouldn't want you to be weeping like this. We have things to prepare. This is Christmas Eve; remember Mama was going to make supper for the homeless children at the mission. Mama would want us to take her place, Papa; she'd want us to be there for the children."

"David, fetch some more coal," Samantha ordered. "The stove is almost burned out. We need to get busy, there's a lot to do before tonight."

Dr. Moyer couldn't believe his eyes or ears. He had expected Samantha would be devastated by her mama's death, and here she was taking charge as though absolutely nothing had happened. And there was a strange aura around her, angelic. The doctor shook his head at the mysterious situation and then picked up the phone to call the rest of the family.

The family began arriving around 10:00. First came Michael with his wife, Jill; John Jr. and his wife, Sandy; followed by the two bachelors, George and Jason. All were sobbing openly, shocked at the loss of their beloved mother, especially at Christmas. Samantha's behaviour surprised them as well as she bustled around acting as though it were just another day.

The mortician, Mr. Judd, arrived at 11:00. He extended the customary condolences, spoke in loud whispers to John, then left, taking Pearl from the home she had lovingly cared for over the past 30 years. Samantha sent her father and brothers to the funeral home to attend to the burial arrangements. Then, with the help of her sisters-in-law, she set about the preparations for the evening meal. Mama's wish would be honoured.

The Reverend Morrison paid his respects in the afternoon and was surprised to see Samantha was going ahead with the children's special supper. He had thought to cancel it, but Samantha took hold of his hand and assured him Pearl would not have wanted that. He left puzzled, but happy to see Pearl was not gone so far away as some might think.

The time arrived to head down to the mission. The children were lined up, waiting for the Henry family's arrival. They had been informed of Pearl's death, and the chapel hall was overflowing with people who come to pay their respects to a wonderful woman.

When the meal was finished, Samantha walked up to the platform. "Tonight is a sad night for all of us," she began. "My dear mama, your precious friend, Pearl, has gone home to her Lord. Many would have expected me and my family to be home mourning, but you need to know that Pearl's greatest desire was for us to be here with you tonight."

The room was hushed except for the odd sniffle. Samantha reached into her pocket, took out the pearl, and held it up. A brilliant light radiated around it. "We must," she paused; "when we see a pearl, remember our own precious Pearl. Even though she is not physically with us, memories of her will live on forever in our hearts and minds. She, like the pearl, was beautiful; her beautiful heart touching each one of us in this room. Pearl always gave unselfishly to those she loved, no matter the cost to her—and she loved you all."

Samantha hesitated and choked back the emotion welling up in her throat. She clasped the pearl tightly in her hand and touched it to her heart. "Everyone, please rise and join me in singing, Angels We Have Heard On High."

The joyous sound of Christmas resounded throughout the hall. Samantha beamed. No one noticed the young girl slip out the back door; no one but the old widow Edna who greeted her with open arms. Samantha fell into those arms, no longer afraid of the village witch. The dam of her sorrow burst.

Later that night as Samantha lay in bed, with her precious pearl tucked beneath her pillow, she dreamed sweet dreams. She dreamed of a gentle old widow named Edna; of a piece of ugly, dirty black coal; of a snow-white pearl, and of a beautiful angel that would be with her always.

The Overdue Letter

(Dedicated to my Aunt, Florence Atkinson)

It was a couple of weeks before Christmas and Mary was going through some recent pieces of writings when she came across a letter she had written while on a writing retreat—a letter she hadn't bothered to send because life had gotten in the way...

Dear Aunt Florence: It has been such a long time since I have written an actual letter to someone—a letter that would travel via the 'snail mail system' as we call it today. When challenged during a writing exercise to think of someone I would like to write to, and then actually write the letter, you were the first person who came to my mind.

Time has flown by so fast, especially these past few years. I missed the festive occasions when the family used to gather at Grandma and Grandpa's house, and we could play with all our cousins. As we got older, we would even have holiday sleepovers. There are times I feel such fragmentation of family, not having seen so many of my cousins for years. I wonder if I would even recognize them if I were to pass them on the street—probably not!

My own children are grown up now, most having left the nest, and I have a much better understanding of what you, my parents, and my other aunts and uncles went through during that time in your lives. I guess it goes to say with just about everything, eh—we don't really know how things are until we actually experience them.

I can still picture your house on Martindale Road in St. Catharines—your garden in the backyard—your warm, inviting kitchen filled with fragrant smells—the front porch where many treasures could be found. I can still see Uncle

Bill in his rocker—I remember the raspy chuckle in his voice as he would smile and say, "How are you, Mary Margaret?" I used to detest it when my aunts and uncles would call me Mary Margaret, but I believe I have finally grown out of that!

I remember your talent with crafts and your generosity when you made those two beautiful dolls for my daughters, and I would like to let you know that they still have them and are proud to say their great-aunt Florence made them.

I have always noted your special love for my father––I've seen the bond there; heard the stories of how no one would dare to harm a hair upon his beloved sister's head if he had anything to do about it!

Those are just some of the memories I have—I'd love to dig up some pictures of us that might jog a few more for me—do you have any? Come to think about it, I should check with Mom and Dad too. I was young then, without a camera of my own. Now I have a digital one and take thousands of pictures, but none are of my precious childhood memories.

I just want to say, Aunt Florence, that even though we don't often say it directly in this fast-paced world we live in, I love you and think about you often. Hope this letter finds you well.

Merry Christmas

Love always, Mary Margaret

Mary folded the letter into an envelope, stamped it, walked to the corner postal box and dropped it in.

A week passed. Mary was busy planning Christmas parties and had finally succumbed to her couch on the Friday night. A steaming cup of ginger-mint tea comforted her tired body. She was just drifting off to sleep when the phone rang.

"Hello," she answered sleepily.

"Hello … Mary Margaret?"

Mary sat up. "Oh, hi, Aunt Florence; how are you?"

"I got your letter today." There was a long pause; neither seeming to know what to say next. Then, "It was nice … don't get many letters nowadays." Another pause. "I dug up some old photos from the albums—nice one of you sitting on your Uncle Bill's lap—you'll have to come here to get them though."

Mary detected tears in her aunt's voice. What had started out as a simple writing exercise for her was ending up as a special moment—one which she should have embraced years ago. Mary smiled into the phone: "I'd love to come and visit with you."

"When?"

"How about Sunday afternoon, weather permitting of course."

"Make it 3:00; I usually nap after lunch."

"No problem; 3:00 – 6 Rice Avenue, right?"

"Yes."

"See you Sunday."

"Do you still like spice cake?"

Mary laughed. "Of course! Especially yours!"

"See what I can do. Bye for now."

The phone clicked off. Mary's heart fluttered. Not only was she going to be walking back down memory lane through her aunt's photo albums, but she was also going to get to have some of her infamous spice cake, as well—this visit was definitely long overdue!

Going for the Red Ribbon

Dedicated to my horse, Star's Joe Sugar

It was the first horse show of the season! There was commotion everywhere as everyone put the final touches on their horses, and then checked their own riding habits— the red ribbon depended on excellence!

"Class number five, confirmation geldings, three years and up, line up in the centre of the ring please."

"Well, this is it, Joe," Joanna whispered. Joe nibbled at her pocket, looking for sugar. She led him into the ring and lined up, placing him in the proper stance for judging. One foot out of place could make the difference between placing or not. Satisfied, Joanna positioned herself on the right side of Joe's head and waited.

"Here comes the judge, Joe; stay still now." Joe swished his tail.

The judge circled around Joe; felt down his legs, along his back and over his shoulders. He even opened Joe's mouth and checked his teeth.

"Walk your horse in a straight line down to the end please, then trot him back." The judge motioned to Joanna.

Joanna led Joe out, and they strolled to the fence. Joanna made a wide right turn so as not to block the judge's view of Joe and then trotted back.

The judge bent down, scrutinizing for any possible faults in the horse's movement.

"Thank you; reposition your horse please."

The judge moved on to the next horse and repeated his routine. He finished the line-up, walked slowly around all the horses again and wrote notes on his papers. One horse sneezed; another flinched at a loud noise. Joe stood still; he was doing great!

"Would numbers: 8, 16, 54, 105, 29, and 3 step forward please? The rest may leave the ring."

Joanna's heart beat faster, and her face flushed pink. She was number 54. She led Joe out behind number 16. Third place wouldn't be bad the first time out.

Once the ring cleared, the judge returned his attention to the remaining six horses. He inspected each horse again, made more notes, and looked again. Numbers 3 and 29 exchanged places. The judge was looking at Joe. Joanna could feel the blood rushing through her veins. She prayed Joe would remain still. Eternity passed. The judge walked around Joe again. He examined number 16 again.

"Number 54, move up one please."

A smile radiated across Joanna's face.

"Results of class number five: first place, number 8, Belair's Dream Boy; second place, number 54, Star's Joe Sugar; third place…"

Joanna slapped Joe affectionately on the neck. "Good boy Joe, good boy!"

Joanna's mom met her outside the ring. "Come on love, we have to hurry; the English pleasure class begins in ten minutes." Her mom smiled, "Second place, eh! Not bad."

Joanna ran a brush quickly over Joe's body. An English saddle was placed on his back, and his halter was exchanged for a bridle and martingale. Joanna slipped into her riding jacket and put on her helmet.

Joanna's dad hooked his hands and catapulted his daughter up into the saddle. "Good luck," he said. "And remember, concentrate on your horse. Don't let the more experienced riders block you from the judge's view."

"Class number 36, open English pleasure, enter the ring please and walk your horses around the railing."

"Here goes, old man." Joanna nudged Joe with her heels. His ears pricked up and he moved slowly into the ring.

The judge stood prestigiously in the centre, watching the horses walk around and around. "Trrr-ot!" the judge commanded.

Joanna kicked Joe into a trot. Around and around they went. The commands kept coming. "Walk your horses … caaa-nter … trrr-ot … walk your horses … turn in the other direction…" around and around and around.

Finally, the judge started picking his possible winners. Joanna concentrated on her posting. The judge motioned her into the centre. Once again, her blood raced through her veins.

More waiting as the judge examined each rider in a stationary position.

"Back your horse … reposition."

Then, around the ring again. This time, Joanna wasn't so lucky. Joe broke his stride when Joanna got him too close behind another horse. They were motioned out of the ring.

"Better luck next time, Joanna." Her dad met her at the gate. "Let's get Joe ready for the barrel race. I'll put the western saddle on while you get changed."

The barrel race was an event Joanna really looked forward to. Joe was fast. He had a long stride. If she kept him close to the barrels, Joe would do the rest on the home stretch. There was no monotony in this class—only anticipation, praying someone wouldn't better your time! A split second could make the difference between the red and blue ribbons!

"Number 54 on deck."

"We're next, Joe. Let's show all these old pros what a couple of greenhorns can do."

Joe tossed his head. He pranced about, yanking at his bit, anxious for his big run to begin.

"Number 54."

Joanna cantered Joe up to the gate. "Let's do it, boy!" Joanna dug her heels into his belly. Joe was off like a shot. Around the first barrel ... a spurt of speed ... around the second barrel ... another spurt of speed to the final barrel at the end ... around they went. Joe's body leaned so far over that Joanna's one foot almost touched the ground. Now for home!

The crowd was chanting: "Go! Go! Go!"

Joanna urged Joe on by screaming, "Yah! Yah!" He flew past the timer!

"That will be a tough one to beat folks—17.52 seconds! Let's have a big hand for the little lady, Joanna Callum, on the big black horse, Star's Joe Sugar."

The crowd clapped their hands, stamped their feet and whistled shrilly. Joanna was elated. She was a success. Even if she didn't take a red ribbon home, the thrill of this race was worth it all!

The drive home was quiet. The hype was over. It had been a fruitful day—a second in the confirmation class, and third in the barrel race. Joanna and Joe had a lot of work to do when they got home—there was another show in two weeks, and Joanna intended on coming home with a red ribbon. "Maybe even a trophy," she thought to herself. "Who knows?"

Fate

It was the usual Saturday night crowd at Sylvie's Tavern. I pulled my stool closer to the bar and threw a toonie down. "Just water tonight, Mike."

"Water? What's wrong with you?" Mike's head tilted inquiringly.

"Been a long week," I answered. "The first thing I really wanted was a double scotch on the rocks; the last thing I really need is…"

"A double scotch on the rocks," Mike finished my sentence as he handed me a bottle of water. "Want a glass with some ice?"

"No thanks," I returned, unscrewing the cap and taking a swig. "Who's playing tonight?"

"Local band—The Midnighters."

"Are they good?"

"Never heard them; boss said to give them a chance and what Sylvie wants…"

"Sylvie gets," I finished for Mike. We both laughed, and he went off to serve another customer.

Time dragged. I sipped my water and watched the local crowd antics. At 9:00, The Midnighters took to the stage. Not one of them looked to be a day over 20, but they weren't half bad, I thought as my foot tapped on the footrest.

"Hey," a stranger clambered onto the stool beside me. "Is this seat taken?"

"No," I replied, turning away from his overwhelming odour.

I heard the man order a whiskey and coke. Then, "Name is Jack," he informed.

I didn't reply.

"You have a name?"

I didn't reply, hoping he would go away.

"I said, do you have a name?" I felt a tap on my shoulder.

"Sam."

"Funny name fer a girl."

"Short for Samantha," I replied curtly, turning away again.

"I done somethin' horrible," Jack stated.

I didn't reply.

"Did you hear what I said, Sam? Give me anotha drink, bartender. Somethin' real horrible; don't know if'n I can live with what I's done."

His voice was getting louder, and I was afraid people would actually start to think I was with him. I reached for my water bottle, ready to make an exit from my stool. Jack grabbed my hand.

"I needs to talk to someone … please."

There was such pleading in his voice and something inside me said, what the heck; why not humour the old drunk? He'd probably pass out in no time anyway.

"Okay, Jack, what is it you have done that is so bad?"

He leaned into me and whispered: "I killed 'im—deader than a doorknob 'e is."

I froze.

"Did you hear me? I killed 'im. Laid 'im out and sliced 'im up."

I shied away, the smell of his whiskey breath making me want to vomit.

"I need you to help me."

I turned back to Jack, keeping a discreet distance, and asked: "Just who did you kill and where is the body?"

"My friend John; well, 'e used to be my friend, but 'e pushed me out 'o my house so 'e ain't my friend no more!"

"Did you live together?"

"No, but 'e was supposed to be my friend. There is supposed to be an understanding out there. He shouldn't 'a done that to me … I had to kill 'im!"

"Where's the body?" I asked.

"In the alley behind the bar."

"In the alley behind the bar?" I echoed.

"Yep, wanna see? I considers you a friend, listenin' to me like this … I kin tell you is a nice person … Sam, isn't it?"

At the point of being called a friend by this man who had just confessed to murdering someone, my stomach churned.

"First of all, Jack, I am not your friend; and I am really not the nice person you might think I am. If what you are saying is true…"

"It's true, Sam; I swears it's true," he pulled on my arm; "I'll shows you."

I sighed deeply. I certainly was not going to go back to a dark alley with Jack—not alone and not without backup. "Sorry Jack," I stood and faced him; "you have the right to remain silent … anything you say…"

Jack's shoulders drooped, and he started to cry, "I thought you was my friend!"

"Maybe in another life," I answered. I took out my cellphone and called the precinct. "Hey, Dan, I need you to send a couple of officers out to Sylvie's Tavern and check out if there is a body in the back alley. I have some drunk here who says he killed someone."

I snapped my cellphone shut. "Mike, can you get Jack another drink; it might be his last for a while."

"Sure, Sam."

"May as well make it a double." Mike smiled, knowingly.

Jack downed the drink in one gulp. His eyes were misty as he grabbed my arm. "You're a good friend," he stuttered. "Best friend I ever had."

Ayla's Angel

Ayla's habit, in the summer of 2006, was to borrow her brother's fishing pole and escape down to the river for a time of quiet contemplation. It wasn't that Ayla really enjoyed fishing, but it gave her a respite from the hustle of everyday life—a life overloaded with responsibilities far beyond what she felt able to handle at times. And she was lonely. Her mother had moved to France—a job transfer—and her brother, Evan, was backpacking in Europe. On top of that, her cat, Misty, had died from some mysterious cancerous tumour.

So it was, on a slightly overcast day at the end of July, that Ayla found herself leaning on a large tree trunk, fishing pole perched precisely between two branches, line floating lazily on the calm river. She was staring dreamily up at the clouds when she heard the laughter. Glancing up to the trail, she saw a group of young boys. One of them was holding a small box, and Ayla heard another boy tell him to just throw it over. She noticed the hesitation in the boy holding the box, but as the others began to chant, throw it over, he finally did. The group laughed and patted him on the back, but Ayla could tell he was not happy about what he had just done.

The box landed not too far from where Ayla was sitting, but she dared not move until the boys left. So far, they were oblivious to her presence. Finally, their voices faded away. Ayla glanced to the trail to confirm they were gone and then made her way over to the box. As she drew closer, Ayla was positive it had moved. She wondered what was inside but was apprehensive about taking a peek. What if it were a snake or a rat?

Gulping down her fear, Ayla picked the box up. It had been duct-taped shut. A scratching sound came from within. She hurried back to her tree trunk and set the box down. The scratching became more insistent and then Ayla heard a meow. She picked at the tape until it gave way. Quickly, she opened the lid. A fluffy, snow-white kitten with bright-blue eyes stared up at her.

"Oh, you poor little angel," Ayla cried as she tenderly lifted the kitten out. "Why would anyone want to hurt you?"

The kitten purred and nestled on Ayla's lap. Ayla reached for her thermos and poured some water into its cup. She then began to place water droplets on the kitten's lips.

"I'll call you Angel," Ayla whispered, "for surely, an angel has watched over you today."

The kitten purred louder.

Angel became Ayla's constant companion. During the fishing excursions, she would roam amongst the rocks, chasing all sorts of river bugs but always staying within close proximity of Ayla. Time sped by; summer vanished, and the misty winds of fall began to crowd the days. Trips to the river lessened, and with winter's first cold blast the fishing trips ceased altogether.

One evening, in early December, a severe storm blew in from the west. The news forecast suggested it was going to last well into the next day. Ayla set out some candles and matches.

"Just in case," she said to Angel, who was rubbing around her legs. "Want a treat?"

Angel ran to the cupboard. Ayla gave her a treat, threw a bag of popcorn in the microwave, and then the two curled up on the couch to watch T.V. Halfway through a movie, the hydro flicked off.

Ayla retrieved her candles from the kitchen. "I guess I'll just finish my book." Ayla looked around. "Angel, where are you, sweetheart?" she called out.

Angel seemed to have disappeared—probably hiding somewhere close. Ayla lit the candles, set them on the end table, and began to read.

"What do you want, Angel ... stop that, you silly cat ... stop your meowing ... I'm trying to sleep ... ouch ... you rascal ... why are you scratching me ... get off my face ... you smell funny ... like smoke ... ouch ... you bit me...

Ayla bolted up! One of the candles had fallen to the floor and the curtains were engulfed in flames. Ayla scooped up Angel and ran out of the house, heading for her nearest neighbour. She banged on their door. She had no idea what time it was.

"What on earth, child!" Mrs. Sims shouted. Then she noticed the flames. "Oh my goodness ... I'll call the fire department!"

Ayla lost everything except her Angel in the fire. Her mom flew home from France to help her settle in a new place. "I guess that was your lucky day," she said after hearing the story of how Ayla had come upon the kitten.

"For sure," replied Ayla. "God sent me as Angel's protector, and in turn, my Angel saved me."

Mother and daughter hugged. Angel jumped onto the counter and blinked her blue eyes.

"Did you see Angel smile?" Ayla's mom asked.

"Yep," Ayla replied as she scooped up her best friend. "All the time."

An Awakening

"In the arms of an angel is where I'll soon be," Sally thought. She sensed something horrific had happened. She was in a hospital room, hooked up to all kinds of equipment. There was a silent, faceless man sitting in the corner.

A nurse, who was taking Sally's vitals, looked worried. Sally tried to say she wouldn't mind being an angel, but her mouth wouldn't open. She tried to touch the nurse's hand, but her arm wouldn't move either.

"Mr. Lukan, I am afraid there is no sign yet of your friend coming out of her coma. Besides the head trauma, there was a massive amount of internal damage."

"Will she recover?"

Why did that voice send shivers up her spine?

"It's hard to say; it has been two weeks since the accident. Some people linger for months before coming out of a coma—some never do."

How could she be in a coma when she could see them so plainly? The man got up from his chair and walked towards her. His scent was repugnant. He was not a friend—of this, she was sure! So why was he here?

He was touching her arm. He was speaking to her, his voice grated on her ears. Where was the nurse?

"How did you manage to live through that fall, Sally? You should be dead. You and your husband have been thorns in my side for years. First, Michael, for promising me something, then dying before he could fulfill his promise—then, you, for being so stuck on him even after he died. It would have been so easy, Sally, if you had succumbed to my romantic advances. I would have married you, looked after you and the brat and had it all—even more than Michael promised!"

Sally could feel the blood rushing to her face. She was married, but her husband was dead. She had a child. Obviously, the brat this man spoke of. And this man must have been a big part of her life. What had changed?

"You must leave now, Mr. Lukan; visiting hours are over," a nurse came into the room.

"Just a few more minutes, please."

"I'm afraid not. Actually, the doctor has noticed a high level of agitation on Sally's monitor whenever you are here, so he suggested you refrain from visiting for a few days."

Sally was relieved this man would be leaving, but he was approaching her again, and he was leaning over her bed.

"Later, Sally; this isn't over yet!" he whispered in her ear. The monitor went erratic. Sally's heart was racing. She felt so helpless. If only she could tell someone her fears! She needed to find out why she was here. She needed to fight her way back into consciousness and remember.

"Poor dear suffered a bad fall. I'll just change this morphine drip..." Sally drifted off, a feeling of euphoria surrounding her...

It was her son Devan's birthday. There were balloons and a big birthday cake on the picnic table. But where were all the children?

Devan appeared excited. He was talking to a man. Sally smiled as she recognized Ryan. Dear Ryan. What would she have done without him after Michael's death?

Ryan was handing Devan a set of reins, which were attached to a dapple-grey pony. "Hey Sally," he called over, "think Michael would approve of his son's new pony?"

"For sure he would, Ryan." She smiled. "Where are all the other children?"

"I sent them home early; I didn't want any of them riding Devan's pony."

"But they haven't even eaten the cake!" Sally wondered at Ryan's strange reasoning.

"No problem; freeze it."

Sally watched Ryan hoist Devan into the saddle. "Take her for a ride, son," he said.

Why was Ryan calling Devan 'son?' He began walking toward her. Sally got an eerie feeling. She shuddered when he took hold of her arm.

"Let's go for a walk; I have something to show you." He led her to the trail which ran along the river bank.

"What about Devan? We shouldn't leave him here alone."

"Boy will be fine," Ryan said, tightening his grip.

Once on the trail, his pace quickened. Sally was about to protest when Ryan said, "It's just over here." He stopped at an extremely narrow section of the trail. There was a drop into a heavily wooded valley which had a river running through it.

"Before Michael got sick he said he was going to give me this valley."

Sally was shocked. Michael hadn't mentioned this to her.

"He died before he could change his will, but he promised me."

"Why is that so important to you, Ryan? And why are you hurting me?" Sally cried as Ryan squeezed her arm harder.

He pulled a sheaf of papers from his jacket. "Sign these papers."

"Why?"

"Willing me that land."

"Why would I do that?"

"You wouldn't want anything to happen to Devan..."

Sally signed.

"Thank you, Sally," he smiled as he swept her into his arms and flung her from the cliff. "Now the gold will be all mine!" Ryan called out greedily.

Sally's eyes opened. "Not in my lifetime!"

Willow House

It was called Willow House after the original owner's wife. James McAndrews had come to Canada from Scotland in 1894 at his brother George's urging. George had written that he had purchased a piece of land just outside a place called Brantford, but he needed help to clear the stone-littered fields. George had also suggested a couple of wives would be in good order as well. James had laughed heartily, for George was quite large and had a roughness to his demeanour that scared the bonniest lassies away! James, on the other hand, was most becoming and had to fight the girls off. Even so, none had ever caught his eye enough for him to wed her—until the voyage to Canada.

She stood on the deck, the wind whipping at her slight body. Her knuckles were white as they grasped the railing. Her long blond hair danced frantically. Her face was freckled from the salty waves' splashes. James could have watched her forever, she was so beautiful. Suddenly an enormous wave surged over the side. The girl was propelled across the deck, but James was there to catch her. As she lay shivering in his arms, he looked down into the most heavenly blue eyes he had ever seen.

"May I take you to your cabin, Miss?" James offered.

"I have none, good sir."

"Then, I shall take you to mine," James said. "James McAndrews at your service."

She smiled.

"Well, girl, do you have a name?" James laughed lightly.

"Willow."

Her eyes closed but James noticed a wince of pain cross her face. "Are you hurt?"

"I shall be fine if you could just help me reach the lifeboat yonder; I have a blanket there."

"You cannot stay out here; a storm is brewing!" James protested. He noticed the gauntness of her face. "When did you last eat, Willow?"

"Before we set sail, but do not worry; I have gone without before," Willow answered. "You must go to your cabin, sir, before you catch your death."

James did not want to let Willow go. His heart throbbed; his blood raced hotly through his veins, and there was a stirring in the pit of his stomach unlike any he had ever experienced. James stood, and with Willow in his arms, he headed for his cabin. She tried to protest, but he pulled her closer to his heart.

"I would just rest a bit and then be on my way," she whispered.

He laid her gently on his bunk and covered her frail body. That was the beginning of their love story.

James kept Willow with him for the remainder of the journey. She told him she was fleeing from her stepfather who had made improper demands on her. She was most grateful to him for giving her shelter. Before the boat sailed into Halifax Harbour, James McAndrews and Willow were wed.

When James presented his bride to his brother, George stated that she was indeed beautiful, but would she be able to do a hard day's work? "Brother," Willow overheard George say, "she seems so frail she will need a maid to see to her!"

"Then I shall get her a maid," James had returned. "No sister or cousin for me?" George laughed.

"Sorry, brother."

There was a pause and then, "What about sons, James? She don't look strong enough to bare a child."

"If we never have a child, I will still know happiness like no other man—Willow completes me, brother."

"Then, so be it."

Willow determined at that moment to never let James down. For the first time in her life, she knew what real love was about.

James and Willow stayed in George's cabin for the first two years of their marriage. In the spring of 1896, James began constructing Willow House.

"It will be grand, Willow my love," he had murmured in her ear as they lay in bed. "On the upper floor I will put four bedrooms, and a fifth room will have a huge copper tub for your baths, and a chamber pot so you won't have to go outside in the cold and dark."

Willow laughed and wrapped her arms around James' neck. She kissed him softly on the lips. "And who shall all the bedrooms be for, my love?"

"For our sprouts, and if we have none, for our friends' sprouts if they have too many. If neither, you may fill the rooms with whatever your heart desires!" James kissed her in return.

That was the night James Jr. was conceived.

It was late November before the house was ready. George had chiselled WILLOW HOUSE into a large stone by the front door. James swept Willow into his arms and carried her across the threshold.

"It is beautiful, James! What did I ever do to deserve you?" she cried.

James brushed away her tears with his lips, "Oh, Willow my love, it is I who does not deserve you."

The winter of 1896 was cold and snowy. The drifts made movement difficult between buildings. To save on firewood, George moved in with James and Willow. "Just until winter is over," he said.

George thought Willow looked paler than usual. "Pregnancy is hard on her," he mentioned to James.

James just nodded knowingly.

Willow was taking a day at a time. The child inside her was constantly moving now. She was tired but still worked hard to make their first Christmas in Willow House as exceptional as possible.

January was as cold and blustery as December had been, but February saw a touch of warmth. Into the second week, Willow began to feel strange, and the baby quieted, barely moving at all.

"I think there is something wrong, James," Willow said one evening. "Is not Widow Johnson a midwife?"

"Heard tell she was," James replied. "You want me to fetch her in the morning?"

"That would be a good idea, I think," Willow answered.

The next morning George headed out to fetch the Widow Johnson. James stayed with Willow. He stroked her forehead. "We shall not be having any more of these sprouts if this is what you have to go through, Willow."

"Women must go through this—it will pass."

Finally, George returned with the widow. She was a husky woman who took charge the minute she walked in the door. "Get a pail of water boiling, boy," she directed at James. "And you," she ordered George, "Fetch some more wood for the fire. This place must be warm tonight for we are going to be having us a baby!"

"But it is too early!" James protested. He glanced at Willow and saw the fear in her eyes.

"When a child decides to be born, you can't stop it! Looks like it has no room in there anyway." She paused. "Where're your linens?"

Willow pointed to a cedar chest. "You must be strong, girl; it'll be over soon."

"I fear something is amiss," Willow whispered.

"Let me see then." Widow Johnson examined Willow. Her brow furrowed with worry. She called to James. "Got any whiskey? The baby is breech, and I'm goin' to have to turn it. Yer wife will need something to dull her pain."

The day dragged into the evening. Widow Johnson turned the baby, but still, the child would not come. The clock was ticking towards midnight. Soon a new day would strike its way in.

James and George sat helplessly outside the room where Willow lay. "Pray with me, George; I cannot lose Willow."

At the moment the clock struck twelve, Willow screamed. "Push, Willow … push," the men heard the Widow order … and then, a cry! They waited for what seemed like an eternity.

Finally, "Come, see your son."

James gazed at the child. He looked frail. "Willow?" he looked questioningly at the Widow.

"Let her sleep. She's weak, but she should pull through. Now, we need to get some food into this baby…"

Widow Johnson took over the household duties. Willow was so fragile it was three months before she could leave her bed and another three before she could do even the slightest task. But, little James Valentino McAndrews, born on February 14, 1897, despite his shaky start, thrived under the watchful eyes of Widow Johnson.

When Willow was well enough, James led her outside and showed her the willow trees he had planted around the house. "I got large branches from Mr. Corning over on Four Ponds Farm. He said if I watered them well, they would be big in no time."

Willow swayed and leaned on James. He drew her closer. "Are you cold, my love?"

"I am never cold in your arms," she smiled up at him.

In the fall of 1897, George and Widow Johnson were married and moved permanently into Willow House. It became a win-win situation for everyone because it was apparent that Willow would never fully recover from the childbirth.

Willow spent the summer days under the sweeping limbs of the willow trees. James Jr. would crawl up on her lap, and she would tell him stories. When he was busy playing elsewhere, Willow wrote in her journal. During the cold months, Willow would sit by the fireplace, sometimes doing needlework, sometimes writing.

On James Jr.'s sixth birthday, tragedy struck. James had gone into Brantford to fetch supplies, and on the way home, a fierce storm blew in. A passer-by thought he heard someone calling for help, but by the time he found James in the gully, he was barely alive.

Before James drew his final breath, he pulled a package from his coat. "Please make sure my wife, Willow, gets this," his voice was raspy. "Promise me."

"I promise."

Willow went silent when she received the news of James' death. "He asked me to make sure you got this, Mrs. McAndrews," the man said, handing her the package.

She took it, turned lifelessly and dragged up the stairs to their room. Inside the package was a gold heart locket with a picture of her and James. She wept, remembering when they had taken that picture—on their first anniversary. Willow put the locket on, lay down on her bed and closed her eyes.

The young woman stood looking down at one of the gravestones in the family plot behind the old farmhouse. "James and Willow McAndrews—In Death, as in Life—Forever in Love—Into God's Arms – February 14, 1903".

"Hello," a voice called out, "I have the papers for you to sign."

"Be right with you." The young woman turned and headed for the house. She fingered the heart-shaped locket around her neck. The tattered journals were clutched under her arm. She touched the sizeable carved stone at the door before stepping inside.

"Sign here, please," the Realtor pointed to several spots. How proud Grandpa James Valentino would be to know Willow House was back in the family, the young woman thought as she boldly signed her name: Willow McAndrews.

Release

The pounding in Jake's head was unbearable. It was a pain he'd had since he was sixteen, five years ago. He took two more painkillers and washed them down with a shot of whiskey. Jake knew he should not do that, but at this point, he would try anything to dull the throbbing. He desired just one hour of uninterrupted sleep.

Jake's eyes closed. His mind wandered back to his sixteenth birthday. Everyone was there: his parents, brother, cousins, aunts, uncles, grandparents and friends—everyone except the one who haunted his dreams. Violet—his beautiful flower, so full of love, laughter and life—so tragically taken before her time—not her fault—his denial.

The psychiatrist said it would be better to forget her, to move on, but Jake needed to speak to her just once more because he felt only she could stop the aching.

"Oh, Violet, where are you?" he whispered into the empty room. "I need to hold you in my arms."

The familiar faces fluttered away, leaving Jake alone on a cliff—the cliff where she had told him everything and where he had promised to love her forever, no matter what. A bright light appeared, and Jake felt a sense of peace as it drew closer and took shape. A hand reached out from the rays, and Jake extended his fingers to touch the fingertips of the shadow. As contact was made, Jake felt a bolt of electricity surge through his body. Before him stood Violet, as beautiful as ever she had been in real life.

"Hello, Jake," her voice was mellow. "How have you been?"

Jake was speechless! Violet floated closer and put her arms around his waist. Her face was so close he could taste the sweetness of her breath. The anguish in his heart finally burst.

"Why Violet ... why?" his voice was raspy with tears.

"I had no choice, my love. I thought you understood."

"Understood what, Violet? We were sixteen."

"I told you everything, remember?"

"I only remember you telling me you were going away and you didn't want to hurt me. You said the sooner we parted, the less pain there would be for both of us."

Violet withdrew her arms and took hold of his hand, "Come, my love, there is something I must show you. Hopefully, you will remember then."

Jake followed her to the edge of the cliff. She pointed downwards. "Look, I have been given this opportunity to show you what my life would have been like had I stayed. I begged the angels to allow me this one request. Hopefully, this vision will release your pain and mine."

"Angels ... my pain ... yours ... what are you saying, Violet?"

"No more talk, Jake ... just look and remember."

Jake gazed into the valley below. Upon a bed of wildflowers was his Violet, but her face was pale and drawn, her skin translucently fragile. Beside her were people in white garments. They were looking at charts, talking and shaking their heads. He was huddled in the corner, head bowed, shoulders shaking. A man in a white coat walked over to him.

"Jake, Violet wishes to speak to you. It is best you come now; she hasn't much longer. The cancer has taken its toll, and it will be a miracle if she makes it through the night."

"But..."

"No buts, Jake; Violet knew she'd be lucky if she saw her sixteenth birthday."

Jake sobbed as he made his way to Violet. "This is not fair." He took hold of her fragile fingers and lifted them to his lips. "Please, my love, you can't leave me today."

"You say that every day, my dearest. I am unable to give you another—it is too hard. You must move on and live your life. Keep our memories in your heart but do not allow them to stop you from living." Violet's voice was so soft that Jake could barely hear her.

"I will not live without you."

"You must." Violet closed her eyes. Her breathing was shallow. Jake lowered his head down and brushed his lips to hers. Violet's breath was cool. "I love you, Jake, forever, but you need to make a new life now. Promise me … promise me…"

Jake's tears flowed freely. He buried his face in Violet's hair and whispered in her ear, "I promise, my love, to love you forever. That is the only promise I will make."

"Jake, if you don't let me go, I am destined to be forever in limbo. If you truly love me, set me free." The picture before Jake faded away.

Jake lowered his head. He understood what he had to do. "My love for you, Violet, is something I cannot stop, but I had no idea your spirit would not rest until I released you. May I have just one kiss before you go?"

Violet's lips brushed his, "Thank you for the release, my love," she whispered and then disappeared into a swirling bright light.

Jake opened his eyes. The headache was gone. He knew there was somewhere he needed to be—today he turned twenty-one, and his family had been waiting a long time for his return.

The Butterfly Dancer

Kalandra remembered the times when she would watch MaraLynne dance in the meadows with the butterflies while she picked wild flowers, which she would dry and make into hair wreaths. Kalandra watched as her young daughter tried to imitate the fluttering movements, and she would laugh as MaraLynne sometimes stumbled and fell down, but then picked herself up and tried again. By the time she was four, MaraLynne had shown the potential to become one with the butterflies she had imitated, and Kalandra decided to seek out Lady Denisia, who was the best ballet teacher in the country. She would figure out some way to pay for MaraLynne's lessons.

"The child is only four," Lady Denisia scowled. "I do not waste my time with infants!"

"But you have not seen her dance!"

"Who has been instructing her up until now?"

Kalandra blushed. "Butterflies," she answered with a barely audible whisper.

Lady Denisia snorted in disgust. "Butterflies! How dare you insult me with such nonsense! I believe this meeting is over!"

Kalandra grabbed Lady Denisia's arm. "Please, I beg of you; just come and watch my MaraLynne ... watch her dance in the meadow by the river ... I shall be there in the morning. Then you can decide whether or not my daughter is worthy of your esteemed instruction!"

Lady Denisia studied the young woman. She noticed the determination; she saw the tears welling in her eyes. She wrenched her arm from Kalandra's grasp. "I shall think about it." With those words, she left the room.

Kalandra went home and prayed for a miracle.

The next morning Kalandra dressed MaraLynne in a simple white frock, fastened a belt of fresh flowers around her waist and placed a wreath in her hair. She held her child at arm's length. MaraLynne's russet eyes stared up at her mother trustingly; her curly auburn locks surrounded her tiny heart-shaped face. She smiled. "Why such a pretty dress today, Momma?"

"It is time for you to look like a butterfly, my love."

MaraLynne giggled and danced out the door.

Kalandra picked her flowers. She kept a close watch on her daughter, and on the road, to see if Lady Denisia would come. MaraLynne had joined a group of fluttering butterflies and was dancing with them. After a time, she tired and laid down in the grass to wait for her mother.

Having finally gathered enough flowers, and not having seen any sign of Lady Denisia, Kalandra retrieved her daughter and headed home.

"Who was the old lady with the cane, Momma?" MaraLynne asked as she skipped along beside her mother.

Kalandra was surprised. "Where did you see the old lady?"

"In the woods over there," MaraLynne pointed.

Kalandra smiled the rest of the way home; she had no doubt Lady Denisia would send her a message.

A week passed before there was a knock on the door. A young man handed Kalandra a note: "I assume you know how to read, miss?"

"Of course," Kalandra replied graciously.

"Then I shall wait here for your reply."

My Dear Kalandra—I have watched your daughter dance and decided my time would not be wasted teaching her the finer points of ballet—please return a reply with my boy if you can attend my home this afternoon for tea so that we might discuss the arrangements of your daughter's training ... Lady Denisia

Kalandra scribbled a quick reply and returned the paper to the boy.

Thus began MaraLynne's formal training with Lady Denisia...

MaraLynne pushed the wheelchair into the theatre and placed it in the front row. She leaned over, kissed the withered cheek of the occupant and noticed the teary eyes. "You are crying, Lady Denisia?"

"Nonsense, child; something in my eye," Lady Denisia returned curtly. "Now hurry, you cannot be late for your debut." She waved MaraLynne away and smiled as she watched her protégé float with the grace of a butterfly as she raced to her dressing room. Lady Denisia was glad she had lived long enough to see this night.

MaraLynne sat for a moment gazing at her mother's picture on her dressing table. "This one is for you, Momma," she whispered as she kissed the glass frame. She then took the walk down the hallway to the stage entrance. She was just in time to hear the announcement...

"Tonight, ladies and gentlemen, we are most pleased to present the opening of an extraordinary performance—'Miss Butterfly'. This ballet was written and choreographed by our very own Lady Denisia; and debuting tonight is our Lady's protégé, Miss MaraLynne. Without further ado..."

MaraLynne fluttered onto the stage ... the crowd clapped thunderously ... Lady Denisia wept tears of joy ... Kalandra smiled down from heaven.

Walk in Our Shoes

A Christmas Story

Jack was ticked off with the hypocrisy of the world! He was angry and frustrated with all the different religions claiming they were the one and only way to some higher order or afterlife. In his opinion, most people could not handle the life they had now!

It was Christmas Eve and Jack sat at home, alone. He had refused the usual invitation to Rebekah and Ian's house for holiday festivities. Who did they think they were anyway? Rebekah was Jewish; Ian was a Christian. And they had invited Anwar, a Muslim, and his wife, Halina, who was Greek Orthodox. Mixed up bunch, in his opinion.

Jack's thoughts turned to Carol's last phone call. Their friends had no idea they were separated…

"Hi, Jack."

"Hello, Carol," Jack answered coldly, not caring for her feelings.

"Rebekah called and asked if we were joining them tonight. They have something special planned."

"Oh, Carol darling—are you asking me for a date? I thought you couldn't stomach the sight of me!" Jack retorted sarcastically. "In fact, I believe the words you used, as you slammed out the door last week, were that I could rot somewhere warm, and as far as you were concerned, if you ever saw me again, it would be too soon!"

"Jack, it's Christmas."

"Bah humbug on Christmas! Is that supposed to mean something to me?"

"It used to. I'd really like to go, Jack—with you. I do miss you. Maybe we can still work this out…"

"You're the one who left, Carol."

"I know," she paused. "Will you reconsider and come?"

"Nope."

"What shall I tell them when they ask where you are?"

"Whatever you want. I don't care about any of them; they're just a bunch of phonies. How can a group of people who can't even marry their own kind expect to know and celebrate the real meaning of Christmas?"

"Do you know, Jack?"

"I really don't care!"

The conversation ended there.

Jack poured another rye and flopped down on the couch. He began flipping through the T.V. channels. Nothing but Christmas shows with songs of glad tidings, families pretending to love one another, Christmas cheer. Wait, here was someone he could relate to—Ebenezer Scrooge, a man like himself, who knew Christmas was just a bunch of hogwash.

Jack stretched out on the couch, "Well, Ebenezer, how say we have a drink together and get to know each other better. We're a lot alike, you and I..."

What the ... where was he? Jack saw Ian coming towards him, but he walked right past him as though he weren't there.

"Anwar, so glad you could make it!" Ian slapped Anwar on the back and handed him a glass of punch. "Rebekah's concoction ... she won't tell me what's in it, but it does go down nicely." The two friends laughed.

Jack reached for a glass, "Don't mind if I do," he said, but his hand went right through the stem.

"No one can see you, Jack."

Jack turned and could not believe his eyes: "Who, or should I say, what the heck are you?"

"I am the Caliph of Consciousness. I am here to show you the error of your ways. Not all on earth is lost."

"Huh … you must not watch the news!"

The Caliph pointed across the room. "Look there—your wife."

Carol was sitting on the couch, surrounded by Rebekah and Halina. She was crying.

"It's okay, Carol, Jack will come around," Rebekah said.

"He's just going through a rough time," Halina added.

"But he has been so bitter lately; he hates everyone!" Carol said. "I didn't want to leave, but I really just can't live with this Jack. I want the old one back."

The Caliph pointed over to where Ian and Anwar stood talking. Their faces had taken on a sombre look.

"I can't understand what has happened to Jack," Ian was saying. "He used to be such an upbeat guy."

Anwar nodded. "Yeah, but lately he is so angry about all the wars and what he believes are hypocrisies in the world. A couple months ago, I heard he blew up at work just because someone's point of view on religion differed from his."

"I didn't think Jack was that religious," Ian said.

"He's not," Anwar informed. "He just likes to argue about it. He has no real clue about what we believe."

"If truth be told," Ian began, "he was pretty upset when you and Halina got married. He confided to me that he liked you okay, but you should have wed one of your own."

Anwar laughed. "He mentioned something similar to me when you married Rebekah!"

"No kidding!" Ian joined the laughter. "Well, maybe Carol is better off without him; she's definitely not his kind. never has a bad word to say about anyone, no matter their ethnic background or place of worship." Ian checked his watch. "Guess we better get going if we are going to make the show on time."

Jack watched his friends and his wife put their coats on and head out the door. "Where are they going?" he asked.

"Do you care?"

"I didn't realize I was that bad; Ian and Anwar are my best friends."

"Ah, therein lays the problem. They were your best friends, and you used to be theirs, but for a long time now you have not respected them for who they are or for whom they married. You set yourself up as judge and jury of their lives and then decided while you were at it, you should tell the rest of the world what was wrong with it as well!" the Caliph admonished. "It is time to re-examine your thinking before you lose everything."

"Lose everything?"

"You've already almost lost Carol, but she still appears to love you, at least who you were—as you heard her say."

The Caliph began to fade.

"Where are you going?" Jack shouted. "How can I turn all this around?"

"I am only your conscience. Another will show you more…" the Caliph was gone.

Jack looked around and realized he was floating around the ceiling of the Sanderson Centre. He felt something brush against his arm.

"Hello, Jack."

"Who are you?" Jack asked, not returning a salutation.

"I am the Rabbi of Rights."

"Why are we on the ceiling?"

"The view and the sound are perfect up here," the Rabbi chuckled. "Oh look, there are your friends and Carol."

Jack looked down. He noticed the empty seat beside Carol. She looked so sad. Then one of his former teachers from Brantford Collegiate walked up to the microphone…

"Welcome everyone," Mr. Jones began. "The senior drama class of Brantford Collegiate decided to do something different this year. They have produced a play in which the main religions of the world are depicted living in harmony. The play was written and directed by three of our own students, each one of them representing one of the religions. Without further ado, I present to you, 'WALK IN OUR SHOES.'

"Like the name of the play, Jack?" the Rabbi asked.

"Huh?"

"Never mind … just watch."

Jack observed in fascination as the students presented faith from different religious perspectives. He noticed how attentive the audience was and that many of the people were dabbing the corners of their eyes.

"I had no idea about the similarities in these religions." Jack turned to the Rabbi. "I guess everyone has the right to believe in their own way without being persecuted."

"Good observation, Jack; now what are you going to do? You have burned a lot of bridges with your prejudice and anger towards your friends and your wife."

Jack was feeling very remorseful now. "What can I do, Rabbi? How do I even face my friends, especially now I know how they feel about me? As for Carol—she deserves better than me!"

"Why don't you give Carol and your friends the right to decide if they want you back in their lives?" The Rabbi was fading away.

"Where are you going? What am I to do now?" Jack called out.

"There is another to show you that..."

Jack was lying in a graveyard. He brushed the snow off of the flat stone. The only words on it were 'Jack Henry—May 1978 to December 2020'. No beloved husband of, or son of, or friend of—no one even cared enough to mark the day of his birth or death!

"Hello, Jack."

Jack looked up. "Who are you?"

"My name is Peter. I am the disciple who denied his Lord when He most needed me. Remember?"

Jack did remember. He had attended church a long time ago—at Christmas and Easter. He also remembered Jesus forgave Peter and had instructed him to build the Christian church.

"All is not lost, Jack," Peter pointed to the grave. "This does not have to be. It is in your power to change it. Follow me." Peter held out his hand.

Jack found himself back at Ian and Rebekah's house, just as his friends and Carol were about to sit down to a meal. He saw them all join hands around the table, and he noticed each was moving their lips in silent prayer.

"They are all giving thanks for the food God has provided," Peter mentioned, "each in their own way, yet all as one."

Jack watched as, after the meal, they gathered around the fireplace in the den and exchanged gifts. He noticed the brave face Carol was putting on.

"There are tears on her heart," Peter said. "Only you can wipe them away."

"I don't think she will ever want to see me again after how I treated her," Jack cried. "As for my friends…" Jack buried his head in his hands. "Oh, what a fool I have been … oh what a fool…"

"God bless us every one, Mr. Scrooge," a child's voice penetrated Jack's consciousness. He opened his eyes and saw Ebenezer skipping joyously down a snowy street with a crippled child on his shoulder.

Jack glanced at his watch. How could this be? It was still only 6:00. There was time if he hurried—if they would open the door to him. Jack dressed and headed out for Rebekah and Ian's house. He hesitated at the door.

"Go ahead, ring the bell," Jack heard a voice say. He turned and saw Carol. He opened his mouth to apologize, but she placed her finger to his lips. "Later, my love, it is enough that you are here," she smiled.

"Jack … Carol … so glad you made it," Rebekah greeted as she opened the door. "Anwar and Halina just arrived as well."

Ian was checking his watch. "We must get going to the Sanderson Centre; we don't want to miss this show. I hear it is the best one the Brantford Collegiate senior drama class has ever performed!"

"What was the name of it again?" Halina asked.

"WALK IN OUR SHOES," Jack answered.

The First Date

Their 50th Wedding Anniversary was coming up soon. Orville and Muriel had decided to return to their hometown of Waterford and see if the little soda shop where they'd had their first date was still there. It had been forty years since they had moved away. Orville had taken a job up in Mattawachan with the Ministry of Environment. It had been a big move for them: their four children had been quite young; one, three, four, and five, but none had started school yet, so that had made a move a bit easier.

Michael, their oldest, had told them they were crazy to make this trip at their age, but they informed him it was of the utmost importance that they did. They did agree to take a train to Brantford (flying was out of the question due to Orville's heart condition), and then they would rent a car for their excursion into Waterford.

They arrived in Brantford on a Friday afternoon, picked up their rental car and drove to the Best Western Hotel; a bit expensive for their tastes. But Michael had insisted and since he was paying for it, his anniversary present to them, who were they to argue. Linda, their oldest daughter, had paid for the train ticket; Sarah and Frankie had chipped in some spending money. It was going to be a great weekend.

Saturday morning dawned with a striking sunrise. They decided to do lunch in Waterford; Orville didn't like driving at night. Besides, the old familiar landmarks of forty years ago might have changed and he didn't want to get lost. Passing through Oakland and Wilsonville generated some old memories—some happy, some not. Finally, they saw the sign—Waterford, Home of the Pumpkin Fest.

Orville slowed to a crawl, despite the impatient young man behind him. After all, the speed limit was 50, and he was only a couple of kilometres under that. He and Muriel focused on the left side of the road. They saw it at the same time—Gram's Café & Deli.

Orville signalled and pulled into the parking lot. The young man squealed his tires as he sped off, glad to be rid of the old couple. Orville found a pull-through parking spot; couldn't be too careful, especially with a rental car. Muriel waited for him to open the car door for her; that's how it had been on their first date. He obviously forgot, so she pressed the horn—once. He smiled sheepishly as he came around and opened her door. There was no second sheepish smile as they entered the café.

Of course, things had changed slightly, but Orville and Muriel found their old familiar corner by the window. It was still there, just a different style of table.

"Hi, my name is Jenny, and I am going to be your waitress today. Could I bring you a menu?" A young teenager stood poised at the end of their table, a pleasant expression on her face.

"That won't be necessary," Orville smiled, and then he described what it was they would like to have.

Jenny grinned. "Yes, we still serve that, sir; it's actually our best seller."

Ten minutes later, Jenny returned with two large glass mugs. Inside was a creamy chocolate pudding with a layer of strawberries one-third the way up, followed by another layer of pudding, a layer of crushed Oreo cookies, more pudding and a topping of rich whip cream adorned with a stemmed strawberry. It was definitely a chocolate lover's heavenly delight! Two long-stemmed spoons were placed beside the mugs.

"On the house," Jenny informed.

"Oh no," Muriel protested.

Jenny smiled and pointed to a gentleman at another table. Orville and Muriel couldn't believe their eyes. It was Mac Johnson, the man who had owned Gram's Café & Deli way back when. Mac smiled and nodded his head to them. "Been a long time," he called over with an authoritative voice. "How are you kids doing?" He stood and walked with a firm step over to their table. "You're looking good."

"Not bad for a couple of old folks, I guess," Orville smirked. "Muriel here has weathered life better than I," he added with a sparkle in his eyes.

"I can see that," Mac laughed. "Well, enjoy your lunch; I have to head home to Maggie, she'll have my lunch ready for me by now. Can't keep her waiting." He turned and left.

As Orville and Muriel dug into their chocolate delight, they reminisced about the long-ago days of growing up in Waterford. They giggled like two young lovers, deep into the afternoon. On their way back to the hotel, the sun was just beginning to dip into the west.

Muriel reached over and placed her hand on Orville's knee. "Best anniversary ever," she sighed contentedly.

"You bet." Orville took one hand off the steering wheel and placed it over his wife's.

Yegor's Gift

Dedicated to my mom, Thelma Cushnie – nee Small

Mr. MacIntyre stood at the front of the class with a sombre look on his face as he told the students about the old hobo, Yegor, who had been found dead, frozen under the bridge the day after Christmas. He noticed the tears in one girl's eyes and decided not to intervene when she fetched her coat and headed out the door of the one-room schoolhouse.

The snow stung Thelma's cheeks as she headed for home. Her tears, which were meant to flood the pain in her heart, froze on her skin. Even though her feet felt like frozen pails of ice, it didn't take long to reach the narrow lake road where she lived. Frigid waves pounded against the forbidden snow banks.

As she ran toward the house, she noticed two sets of footprints heading out. Good, both Mother and Dad were at the barn. Thelma ran inside. The smell of bread baking in the wood cook stove greeted her. That meant mother wouldn't be gone long. She headed up to her room, taking the stairs two at a time, and threw herself on the big bed she shared with her little sister, Donna.

The warmth of the goose-down comforter melted her tears, but the pain in Thelma's heart didn't dissipate. Why Yegor? Some of her classmates made fun of him: his name, the way he dressed, his accent, the fact that he lived under the bridge. But she knew better; he was her friend. Thelma glanced over at the two wooden figurines on her dresser and dreamed back to the day she'd first seen him...

She had been ten that summer and was in the front field picking strawberries with her sister, Francis. Donna, under the watchful eyes of big sisters, was playing with her doll under the walnut tree. Thelma saw him first. He was ever so tall and wispy thin. His scraggly grey beard and hair blew wildly in the summer breeze. His faded clothes were covered in patches, and he was shoeless. A wooden stick, holding a sparsely bulging burlap sack, rested on his left shoulder.

"Francis, look," Thelma pointed to the hobo.

Francis looked up just as the hobo turned into their lane. She'd sprang into action. "You get Donna and head to the house," she ordered. "I'll run to the orchard and tell Dad."

Thelma had dropped her berry basket, raced to where Donna was, grabbed her hand and headed to the house. Donna's doll was left behind. Mother had been startled by their hurried entrance.

"What's going on?" she had asked. "And why is your sister crying, Thelma?"

Thelma's words had gurgled out: "An old hobo is coming up the laneway. He looks terrifying. Francis ran to get Dad."

Bertha had peeked out the window. "It's okay, girls. That is Yegor. Your dad met him in Vineland yesterday. Since Marvin left to nurse his sick wife, dad needed to hire someone. Most farm workers have already found positions by this time of year; dad was lucky to get him."

"But he looks so old," Thelma had protested.

"I believe he is," her mother had agreed. "But, apparently he knows a lot about farming."

"That's a funny name—Yegor," Thelma had wrinkled her brow.

"It's a Russian name," her mother informed. Bertha had headed for the door. "Thelma, take your sister to get her doll; I'll direct Yegor to the orchard."

Thelma hadn't actually met Yegor personally until a few days later. One morning as she was exiting the barn, her head down, being watchful of the apron full of eggs, she had bumped into him. "Oh, I am so sorry, sir," she'd stuttered.

He'd smiled as he quickly caught an egg trying to escape the apron. He placed it gently back with its friends. Thelma had noticed how gnarled his fingers were and wondered how he could work with them.

"Thank you, sir." Thelma had been shaking scared.

"Name is Yegor," his voice was gentle.

"I know, sir."

"You may call me that then," he had smiled again, and Thelma noticed his white teeth—strange—she had thought they would be broken and brown like the hobos in one of her books. She smiled back.

A few days later, Thelma had been in the orchard picking up the fallen cherries when Yegor jumped out of one of the trees and startled her. She had stepped back, tripped over a tree root and fell on her behind! He had laughed. A soft laugh. Not mocking.

"Be careful, little miss," he had said as he helped her up.

"My name is Thelma!" she had answered.

They had stood staring at each other. Thelma noticed how startling blue his eyes were beneath the bushy black eyebrows. Then they had burst out laughing, and the bond of friendship began.

Thelma followed Yegor around for three summers, helping him and learning from him. He had told her his Russian name translated to George in English and that it meant farmer or earth-worker. He had said he had always worked on the land, even in his beloved Russia. He told her he had come to Canada with his wife, Katia, and daughter, Klara, when he was thirty. Klara had been ten and Thelma reminded him a lot of her. Tears seared his words as he told her how his beloveds had died of a horrible fever two winters after their arrival in the new country, shattering his heart.

Yegor had shown her how to prune fruit trees and grape vines; how to stack hay on the wagon so it wouldn't slip over the side; how to hold the reins so as not to tug too hard on the horses' mouths, while still keeping them under control; how to hoe earth around vegetables to keep the sun from burning the roots; how to pick delicate fruits so as not to bruise them; how to carve beautiful things from wood, and oh, so much more.

She remembered the extra cold nights when he would sometimes sleep in their haymow, and how she had snuck treats out to him and then he would tell her stories. Thelma loved his stories, especially "The Nutcracker and the King of Mice." Her favourite part was where the Nutcracker turned into a prince and took Clara on a journey to the Land of Snow, an enchanted forest. Yegor would then hum a song as he showed her how to waltz.

Yegor was proud of the Russian connections to the story—A. Vsevolozsky, a director of the Imperial Russian Theatres who commissioned chief ballet master, Marius Petipa, to choreograph the ballet. He, in turn, commissioned Peter Tchaikovsky to write the musical score, and then when Marius took ill, his assistant, Lev

Ivanov, took over the choreography. "The Nutcracker" had premiered at the Maryinsky Theatre in St. Petersburg on December 18, 1892.

Thelma got up and retrieved the two wooden figurines to her bed. Gently, she ran her fingers over the smooth curves of the carved wood. Sobs wretched their way to the surface once again as she remembered the past Christmas…

Dad had let Yegor and her take the team and sleigh to go cut the Christmas tree. She had put the harness with the Christmas bells on the horses. Thelma had held the reins just right as they headed across the fields towards the woods at the far end of the farm. They knew which one they wanted, having discovered it during one of their Sunday summer walks.

Thelma had frowned as Yegor coughed while cutting down the juniper. She worried even more on the return home, for his cough worsened, and when she glanced back at the tracks, she noticed the trail of blood. She had made sure to tell her mother, and she, in turn, had insisted that Yegor spend the holiday time with the family.

"After all, you are like family now," she had said; "I insist." Yegor had smiled, but it was a weary smile. Thelma could tell something was dreadfully wrong with her friend. He had helped her, Francis, and Donna decorate the tree, especially the upper branches, and then he had pulled a wooden angel from his coat pocket and set it on the highest peak before leaving for the barn. Thelma had headed upstairs to her room to finish colouring his Christmas present: a picture of the Nutcracker Prince and Clara dancing in a barn. She had drawn a hole in the roof, allowing star-shaped snowflakes to fall all around them.

A snowstorm blew in on Christmas Eve. Bertha had made delicious chicken soup for supper that night, saying that they would feast on Christmas Day. But Thelma suspected her real reason for making the soup: Yegor's cough had worsened over the week. The family had sat around the table after supper and sung Christmas carols while Bertha played the Hawaiian guitar. Yegor had just sat in the old rocker by the cook-stove, smiling at the joy around him.

"Well, children," their dad had stood up when the clock struck 9:00, "off to bed or Santa may not come!"

The girls hugged their parents, and then Francis and Donna headed upstairs. Thelma lingered a moment longer to give her friend a hug. "You will be here tomorrow, won't you?" she had questioned, looking deep into his eyes.

Yegor had taken her small hands in his and kissed the back of each like a prince would do to a princess. "Of course," his voice was raspy. When he hugged her, Thelma heard the rattle in his chest.

Before getting into bed, she looked at the picture she had finished for Yegor and just knew he was going to love it. But Christmas Eve was the last time Thelma had seen Yegor. He hadn't shown up on Christmas morning, afternoon, or evening. He had just disappeared. However, there had been an extra present under the tree for Thelma on Christmas morning. Two painted wooden carvings—the Nutcracker Prince and Clara.

A gentle knock came on the door, and Thelma's mother entered. She saw the state her daughter was in, sat down on the edge of the bed and drew her into her arms. "They are beautiful," she whispered into her hair.

Thelma nodded. Then she got up, went to her dresser and opened the top drawer. "I didn't get to give this to him," she sniffled, handing her mother the picture.

Bertha smiled. "This is beautiful, Thelma. How say we talk to your dad and see what we can do about making sure Yegor gets your gift?"

That day, after lunch, Thelma's dad hooked up the team, and they drove into Vineland. He pulled up in front of the funeral parlour. Thelma looked at him, wonderingly. "The funeral is today," her dad said.

They were the only ones there besides the funeral Director and the Anglican minister. Yegor lay asleep in a plain wooden casket. Thelma approached him, her dad following close behind. She stepped up on the box provided for children and peered down upon her friend, noticing the recent worry lines had all disappeared. Carefully she took the picture out from inside her coat, leaned over, and placed it gently beside her friend.

"Merry Christmas, Yegor," she breathed into the silence. A tear fell onto the old man's hand. "And thank you for your gift; I shall treasure it always."

Return to the Sea

The smell of salt water was strong in Muirin's nostrils, and she felt strangely calm.

"Not long now," Conall informed as he turned the car onto a gravel lane.

Muirin was nervous. She had never met her great-grandmother. Sending her to Ireland had been her father's idea. "I want you to meet yer great-grandmother Keelin afore she passes on," he had said, Irish still in his words. "She knows our family history and I 'ave bin thinkin' it is time to record the truths along with a wee bit o' the tales. Since you want to be a writer, maybe you kin begin with a story that 'as yet to be told?"

"Well, 'ere we are," Conall stopped in front of a large, rambling frame house.

Bushes grew wildly up the paint-chipped boards, some even covering the windows on the ground level. A tall, elderly woman opened the front door. "Muirin, welcome to my home," the voice was warm and musical.

Muirin received a hug and was ushered inside. The foyer smelled of the ocean. She glanced around—shells were everywhere.

Keelin smiled, "You like my shells?"

"They are beautiful, but why so many?"

"They make me feel at home. Come, child." Keelin hooked her arm through Muirin's and led her into the sitting room. "Conall," she said, turning to him for a moment, "please put Muirin's things in the guest room."

Keelin returned her attention to Muirin and smiled. "I am so happy you have come. I have a story to tell you." Keelin examined Muirin's hands. "They are like mine, I see."

Muirin had always been embarrassed by her hands, for between each finger was a thin web.

"Do you know what your name means?" Keelin asked.

"No."

"Born of the sea."

Muirin laughed. "Is that why I have webbed fingers and flat feet—to propel me through the water?"

Keelin smiled, "Yes, and now it is time you knew the rest of the story... My great-great-grandmother, Muirin, was a Merrow; in modern terms, a mermaid. You are the first female in our line to be given her name.

"She was the most striking Merrow in the ocean, and many sailors wanted to capture her for their own, and for the possible wealth she might bestow on them from plundered shipwrecks. For years Muirin evaded them. As many Merrows do, she swam amongst the seals for camouflage; her own cloak being made from the finest sealskin!

"One day, a hurricane hit the coast, and Muirin was swept up onto the rocks here at Rossan Point. It was there my great-great-grandfather, Aidan O'Sullivan, found her unconscious and with an enormous gash on her forehead.

"Aidan was well aware of the tragedy which could befall his family if he kept a Merrow, but she was so beautiful he could not take his eyes from her. He brought her here to this very house, took her sealskin cloak, hid it well away, and then tended to her wounds.

"When Muirin awoke, she was furious that her cloak was gone. But then, something unusual happened—she fell in love with Aidan, for he was a man of good heart. She would sometimes stand on the cliff, dreaming of her ocean waters, but then she'd touch her belly, where grew the seed of their first child, and she'd turn around and go back to the arms of her Aidan. They had three daughters: Aishling, Tanai and Siofra.

"Muirin's cloak and its secrets have been kept hidden from those who would not understand. I am too old to use it now, but you may try it on if you like," Keelin pointed to a wardrobe in the corner. "It's in there."

Muirin was nervous, yet curious. What would it feel like to wear her ancestor's sealskin cloak, especially if it were that of a real Merrow? She opened the wardrobe, reached in and touched the fur. A tingling spread from her fingers into her body. She lifted it out and slipped it on—a perfect fit.

"I must rest now," Keelin said. "Take a walk if you like. There is a path that goes down from here to the shore. The cloak will keep you warm."

"Thank you, I think I will stretch my legs."

Keelin watched Muirin walk to the cliff and then down to the ocean. She watched as her great-granddaughter stepped into the water and dove into the waves. She picked up a pen and paper, and wrote the letter she knew must be written:

Dear Craig: Muirin asked me to write to you and tell you she will not be home for a while. She says she feels at home here with the ocean waves so close by. I hope this is not a problem for you; I will take good care of her. Thank you so much for allowing her to visit … Your loving grandmother, Keelin.

The smell of salt water was strong in Muirin's nostrils. She felt strangely calm as she dove deeper, the cloak guiding her into a new world.

Peter's Father

Cat's in the cradle and the silver spoon/Little Boy Blue and the man in the moon/When you comin' home, Dad?/I don't know when/But we'll get together then, son/You know we'll have a good time then...

The old Harry Chapin song haunted Peter's mind as he stared at his father. "Well, I guess we have finally gotten together, eh, Dad," he mumbled.

"He did love you," a grey-haired lady whispered.

"You really think so?"

"He didn't know what to do. We were young, and he was such a free spirit. He just couldn't settle to married life."

"You were young, too, Mom. Younger than him. You didn't abandon me," Peter commented sarcastically.

"It's different for a woman," melancholy clutched her words.

"Shouldn't be!" Peter turned away from the coffin. He noticed a middle-aged woman in a corner. She was dabbing her eyes. "I wonder who that is?" he asked, pointing to the corner.

His mom shook her head. "I don't know."

Peter walked over to the woman. "Might I ask who you are, ma'am?"

She gazed up at Peter through misty eyes. "You must be Peter; you look just like Frank," she smiled and offered him her hand. "I am a friend of your father."

Peter ignored her offered hand. "A friend?"

"Actually, I've been your father's companion for the past 25 years."

"Oh ... companion." Peter's mouth curled mockingly. "Funny, he never mentioned you. Oh, excuse me; he never really mentioned much of anything to me! He couldn't commit to you either, eh?" Peter turned to leave.

The woman grabbed hold of his hand. "Please, I'd like to see you after the funeral. I have something for you from your father."

Peter pulled away. "I don't want anything from him. It's too late for him to give me what I really would have wanted!"

"Don't judge so harshly; he did love you."

Peter snickered.

"So said my mom."

"He loved her too."

"Oh, he loved her so much that he left her with a child and never looked back!"

"I won't defend him for that, but I think you need to see what he has left you and then decide for yourself."

"I don't want to give him the time of day." Peter started to walk away. "I am only at the man's funeral to appease my mom."

"Here's my business card if you change your mind."

Peter shoved it in his pocket and headed for the door.

Peter stayed with his mom for a week after his father's funeral but now it was time to get back to his life. He couldn't understand why she still loved the man; why she just hadn't remarried and gone on with her life. His father had indeed moved on! Peter reached in his pocket for his keys, and his fingers brushed against the business card. He pulled it from his pocket ... Kyla Morrison, Artist, P.O. Box 295, Brantford, ON ... 519-555-7686. "Maybe I should call and see what this is all about," he mumbled.

"See what what is all about?" His mom was standing in the doorway.

"Nothing."

"Peter, you were never a good liar."

"Must take after you then, Mom; my father certainly knew how to lie!"

"Your father never really lied to me, Peter; he just wasn't ready for a family. He was overwhelmed when I got pregnant; we were only eighteen. I think once he left, he was too ashamed to come back."

"Why do you always make excuses for him, Mom? He left and didn't look back. He shacked up with another woman. Did he bother to contact you to see if we were okay? Did he even care about me?"

"Your grandpa told me he came to the hospital when you were born but wouldn't stay."

Peter's face clouded with anger. "Face it, Mom … he didn't really give a damn for either of us! He'll not have my sympathy just because he died!" Peter grabbed his suitcase, pushed past her, and headed for the front door. He got in his car and spun out the driveway.

He drove to Waterworks Park and stopped his car at the end of the roadway where the trails began. He got out and walked into what he had nicknamed The Pine Forest, found a fallen tree trunk, sat down and wept.

A couple with a little boy were heading his way. The boy was talking excitedly to his daddy. Peter noticed the father pointing things out on the trail. The mother was laughing as she watched. Peter's heart thumped; why couldn't he remember a walk in the forest with his parents? "Oh right … you left me, Dad!"

He stood up, took out the business card and dialled Kyla's number on the way back to his car.

"Hello, Kyla here."

"This is Peter; I'd like to come over and pick up whatever my father left me. Where do you live?"

Kyla told him her address. "See you shortly."

Kyla showed Peter the three-season room where she painted. He was impressed with her work. Her easel stood on a rotating platform. "Your father built this for me so that when I painted, no matter what time of day it was, I could capture the perfect lighting."

"What did he do for a living?"

"Actually, he didn't work. He had an accident which left him with some permanent brain damage; he had constant blackouts and severe mood swings. His insurance settlement was quite substantial, so he was able to invest the money and live off the proceeds. He needed something to do, so I suggested he take up photography. He'd tried painting, but the accident also left him with what he called a spontaneous handshake."

Peter followed Kyla into another room. The walls were lined with photographs: the Grand River, the trails, scenic settings, and people going about their daily affairs. Peter turned serious. "You know, I am thrilled he had a good life. I guess he didn't think to forward any of his windfall to my mom. She struggled to make ends meet, sometimes even working a second job. I'm still paying off my student loan debt. No excuse in the world will let me forgive him for his lack of support!"

"I'm not asking you to forgive him. Many people have regrets when they are dying, and sometimes those regrets are too late, but..."

"Well, he can certainly consider himself too late!"

Kyla left the room. She returned with a box. "This is yours; do with it what you will."

Peter took the box. "I'll be going now; I'd prefer to open this in private—if I open it at all."

Kyla nodded in understanding and walked Peter to the door.

Peter set the box on his workbench. Inside were several photo albums. Lying on top of them was a letter...

Peter, I know if you are reading this, it is too late for me to make amends in person. Call me the gutless wonder—call me what you like—I know there is no excuse for what I did to you. Not a day went by that I did not think of you, but I admit to being a coward. I'm not asking for your forgiveness—I don't deserve it. I am giving you these photo albums of pictures I took of you. I was there, in the distance, capturing moments of your life on film. It was all I had of you—more than I deserved.

I have watched you with your son. You are a great father, Peter; I am proud of the man you have turned out to be. Your mother did an excellent job—and your grandfather. I saw him always in your life. Even though it probably means nothing to you at this point, I am sorry...

There was no signature, and the writing was exceptionally frail. Peter flipped through the photo albums. Pictures of him at the park with his mom and his grandpa, playing in his backyard, in the schoolyard, at his soccer and rugby games, out with his friends, his wedding day, of him exiting the hospital with his son, Jason, in his arms, of him and Jason at the park...

"He was a regular peeping tom," Peter mumbled as he closed the last album and returned it to the box. "You were a heck of a photographer; too bad you couldn't have been as good a father!"

Peter took the box, placed it on the top shelf in the storage room and went upstairs. "Jason! Time to go to the park, son! Shall we pick up great-grandpa?"

"Yeah!" Jason came bounding out of his room and leapt into his father's arms. "Can I go down the big slide today, Daddy?"

"You sure can, son; you sure can."

Grandpa's Story

Dedicated to my Grandfather, George Cushnie

It was on a Labour Day that Catherine's grandpa had told her his story, and since then, she always spent that day with him.

She retrieved a small box from her dresser drawer. "To our special place we go," Catherine whispered, placing the box in her pocket. Tears crept down her cheeks. How she missed him.

Catherine headed out the door with her cassette player. From the main river trail, she branched off to "their special place." She settled on a log, took a cassette from the box, placed it in the player and pushed "on"…

"Are you sure you want to tape this, Catherine?"

"I don't want to miss a word of your story, Grandpa."

"Not so different from many others."

"It is for me because it's yours."

Laughter…

"Ask away, Catherine."

"What are your first memories of life, Grandpa?"

"I have a faint memory of a beautiful woman, I presume my mother, rocking me in a huge old rocker. And then I am in a barren room. There is a cot with a tattered blanket, a timeworn dresser, and a small window, high up, which I try to look out of, but I am too small. I feel cold and hungry—always cold and hungry."

"Where was this?"

"The orphanage."

"Orphanage? Why, Grandpa? What happened to your parents?"

"My mother died giving birth to my baby sister. My father was devastated; he couldn't handle losing her, or the responsibility of eight children, so he left us in the care of his parents. I have no memories of him."

"What happened to your brothers and sisters?" Catherine remembered her grandpa's voice had been riddled with pain as he began this part of his story...

"The baby was adopted out. My sisters were sent to homes to learn housekeeping; my brothers to various tradesmen. I was too young for apprenticing, and eventually, I was sent to an orphanage. That's how things were done then.

"That is where I spent my childhood. New kids were always the subjects of the senior boys' malicious pranks and I quickly learned to defend myself. It was nothing like the childhood you knew. We were always working. The youngest had to scrub the floors, bathrooms, and dishes."

"How long were you there, Grandpa?"

"Ten years. By the time I was 12, I had the carriage of a man and I joined the fold of the older boys."

"I can't imagine you hurting anyone though, Grandpa."

"Oh, I couldn't be mean, and once I was part of them, things changed. I convinced most to leave the young boys alone."

Catherine knew what was coming next ... she had broached a touchy subject, and her grandpa's eyes had teared as he conveyed his heart's burden...

"It never happened to me personally, not that there'd been no attempt by a couple of older boys when I first arrived; but there was one headmaster—Mr. Collins—and there was evil in his eyes and an insatiable hunger on his lips when he gazed at the young boys. Jimmy was his first victim. We found him bleeding in the washroom one morning, but when we asked him what happened, he refused to say. As time passed, we older boys knew, because there were others. We celebrated the day Mr. Collins disappeared."

"What happened to him?"

"No one really knows for sure…"

Catherine could have sworn her grandpa had smiled when he revealed that fragment…

"Getting back to my story, due to my immense stature, I was put to learn blacksmithing. I could pick a large dinner plate up with this hand."

Grandpa had held out his hand to show her the enormity of it, even at his age.

"The year I turned 16, I was sent to Canada via the Home Children Program. My apprenticeship was finished, and there wasn't a horse around I couldn't nail a set of shoes on! A horse farm on the outskirts of Brantford needed a Smithy, and the orphanage headmaster felt I would be ideal for that position.

"They are a fine Christian family, he told me, and it will only take you five years to pay off the passage money. It is a land of opportunity for those who are not lazy, and once your dues are paid, you can find yourself a bride and make a family.

"The next day, I was on the boat to Canada. We landed in Halifax and from there I took a train to Brantford. I thought the journey would never end! When I met my benefactor, I got a real bad feeling—he had a headmaster Collin's look about him.

"His wife was nice, though. She insisted I attend church with her every Sunday; I never objected because it was my only time off. They didn't have children of their own … not sure why.

"I thought those five years would never end. I worked from before sunrise until long after sunset. There were over 50 horses to tend most times, and Mr. Michaels treated his horses better than he did humans … never stinted on anything for them, so when he demanded top dollar, he always got it."

"How old were you when you left there?"

"I was 21. The old man tried to say I'd eaten too much, so I still owed him, but I'd kept good track of the days. I had no idea where I was going or what I would do, but I was a survivor, and I had a trade.

"Mrs. Michaels gave me some money … said it would tide me over till I found a job. She advised me to get a room at the YMCA on Queen St. I gave her a hug and thanked her for all her kindness."

"How far was it into town, Grandpa?"

"About five miles. One of the neighbours was headed to Brantford for supplies, and he gave me a ride. Nice man. Actually, a boy from my orphanage had ended up on his farm. Donald. Sometimes, we'd sneak out on Saturday nights and meet by the river. We knew we could catch up on our sleep during the Sunday morning services!"

Grandpa's laugh mingled with the forest sounds. Catherine wiped her tears. She'd had no idea how tough things had really been for her grandpa. She put the next tape in.

"How did you meet Grandma?"

Catherine pictured her grandpa's smile…

"Your grandmother was the prettiest girl at the dance. All the boys had eyes for her. We'd line up on one side of the gym, and when the music began, the boys would walk across and pick a gal.

"I didn't get to dance with her until the fifth dance. I saw her shake her head at Rolly, and then she looked over at me…"

The tape kept rolling. Grandpa elaborated on his courtship and his marriage. He had taken any job he could to make ends meet. On market days, he used to go down to tend the farmers' horses' feet, and he would get food in exchange for his services. Word spread about what a good Smithy he was. One day, a local blacksmith called on him.

"Hubert just knocked on my door and offered me a job. He had no family and was getting too old to handle the rambunctious steeds. I was with him for five years; your dad and Uncle James were born then. When Hubert passed away, he left me the business.

"I had to travel a lot though, and when your grandma's lungs went bad, I took a job at Massey Harris— sold the blacksmith business to Donald. He did well—drove a big Lincoln when he retired. By this time, your grandma and I had six children. Lost one—Catherine—that's who you were named for…"

"What was your worst time, Grandpa?"

Catherine remembered the firm set of his jaw as he embarked on his journey through the Dirty Thirties.

"We fared better than some. Your grandma baked the best bread a man could sink his teeth into. When I was laid off from the factory, we'd bake all night, and then I'd go out in the morning with one of the boys and deliver the bread."

"Dad used to tell me you would say not to collect at that house because an old widow lived there, or not to collect at that house because it was a large family and the father was out of work…"

"Times were difficult for everyone then, the community had to pull together. God blessed us—not with plenty, but with necessities. Folks today have too much. All their gadgets don't really make them happier."

Catherine listened as her grandpa told stories of his children and of her birth…

"And then there was the day you were born, Catherine—my first grandchild. I was thrilled. My son had a child, and she would never experience the hardships I had. She would have a good solid family foundation with aunts and uncles, and eventually lots of cousins to grow up with."

Finally, Grandpa recounted her grandmother's final days. He had been calm, even as his eyes brimmed with tears…

"She was my life. You are a lot like her, and it does my old heart good to see how you have taken charge to arrange family reunions every year."

"I think next year I'll suggest we camp at Brant Park so we can spend more time together. I'll rent a trailer, Grandpa, and you can bunk with me."

"The thought is wonderful, Catherine, but I am afraid I won't be here next summer. I have cancer, and it's already spread to my liver. The doctors say I'll be lucky to see Christmas."

He'd made it to Easter. Catherine had woken up at 2:30 Easter morning … and she knew…

"Don't you be crying at my funeral, Catherine; I've had a good life—celebrate it. Know I am at peace with God. Promise me this, Catherine…"

"I promise, Grandpa."

Catherine sat a few moments more before heading for home. She stopped at Wilkes Dam. Grandpa had liked to take a little rest there before heading up the hill to the trail, and then to his home on Dufferin Avenue. It was her home now.

A couple of fishermen waved to her. She recognized Bart and Victor, her grandpa's old buddies.

"Been with your grandpa, Catherine?" Victor hollered.

"You bet, Victor."

"How is the old fellow?" Bart called.

"Fair to middlin', but more fair than middlin', I'd say," Catherine laughed.

"You take care, Catherine. See you in a bit. Man builds a terrible hunger fishing, you know."

"The table will be set at 5:00 ... don't you two be late!"

When Catherine arrived home, she placed the tapes back in their drawer. They would stay there until next Labour Day. She smiled and then went downstairs to prepare supper. Tonight, there would be four plates at the table, and her grandpa's life would be honoured once again.

In Remembrance Of

Dedicated to my grandfather, Alexander Beaumont Small

The silence brought many memories back to Alexander Beaumont Small. He wondered how many of the people who gathered at this Cenotaph understood what it was like to fight in a war. He opened his eyes and studied the group of high school students. He had never gone to high school; there was too much work to be done on the farm.

He and his brothers, Bob, Henry, and Charles, had been taught advanced figures by their father. They were also expected to study from the history books their mother, Eliza, had brought over from England. Of course, Sunday was the Lord's Day, and if you read anything, it was His Word.

Beau, as he had been called from an early age, focused on a young man standing by the mayor. The youngster reminded him of himself in 1914, 80 years ago. Beau had been full of life then; full of hope, full of future. The young man had the same sandy-blond hair and the same serious look in his blue eyes.

Beau had not missed a Remembrance Day service since he had retired, but after each one another level of sadness enveloped him, for he could see where the world was headed. At times he felt all he had fought for had been in vain.

Beau remembered the day it was announced Canada was at war. Henry was already married and Charles was only eight. He and Bob would enlist in a couple of years if the war lasted that long. He remembered how excited they had been to get over to Europe and push the German army back into Germany. It was an excitement that was short-lived once they were there.

A tear slid down Beau's cheek at the memory of his friend's funeral last month. Felix Eichmann. He and Felix used to talk a lot about the war, especially lately as the world was becoming so volatile. They had feared for their grandsons for they knew another world war would be so much worse than the one they had fought in. The one that had haunted them over the years. The one that had left not only external scars but internal suffering—some spoken of, some not.

The sound of the Taps reverberated into the silence. He watched as people began to head for their cars. He watched as the uniformed groups, carrying the country's flags, formed an Honour Guard for the town dignitaries as they exited off the stage. He watched the school children pile into the waiting buses. They would return to school and talk some more about the war—today. Beau watched and waited. His daughter, Donna, would be along soon to take him home. She'd had a doctor's appointment this morning and had not been able to attend the ceremony.

"Are you okay, sir?" Beau looked up and saw the young man who had been standing by the mayor.

"Yes, son, I am fine."

"Is someone coming for you, sir?"

"My daughter," Beau replied, "but she's running a bit late."

"There is a coffee shop across the street, sir; I could wait there with you until she arrives."

"Might not see her," Beau replied. "I lost an eye in the war, and the other one is not so good either … cataract, I think."

"If you tell me what kind of car she is driving, I will watch out for her," the young man offered. "In the meantime, we can have a hot drink, and maybe you can tell me some war stories."

"Maybe."

Beau stood and followed the young man. His cane served two purposes: it kept his balance and informed people he had a problem with his sight. "She has a little red Honda," he mentioned on the way across the street. "Do you have a name, son?"

The young man blushed. "Oh, yes ... Robert," he said as he opened the coffee shop door.

Beau smiled. "Good name. My brother's name was Bob. We fought in the war together, you know; it was good to have my brother with me. You can call me Beau."

They made their way to a seat in the corner. "Could I get you something?" Robert asked.

"A black tea and an oatmeal-raisin cookie would be nice," Beau replied.

Robert fetched the tea and cookie for Beau and a coffee for himself.

"Drink a lot of coffee, son?"

"Not really; two a day is my limit." Robert sat down. "When did you enter the war, sir?"

"Beau ... I enlisted on March 1, 1916, as soon as I was old enough. Had to be sixteen. My brother, Bob, was only ten months older than me, so he waited till I could sign up."

"What battalion did you fight in?"

"20th. It was the Central Ontario volunteers; Bob and I were part of the 44th Lincoln and Welland Regiment. Most of us were just volunteers wanting to defend freedom and our homes. Most from our area were farmers with no actual fighting experience. England called upon Canada—Canadian boys answered.

"Bob and I arrived in France in the Spring of 1916. The troops had spent the winter battling lice, trench foot, and disease. We were assigned to the 4th Brigade and expected to retake the craters near the village of St. Eloi that the 6th Brigade had been forced to fall back from. We managed to retake one crater and hold on to it despite a month of constant shelling. Big loss of life, though."

"Were any of them your friends, sir?"

"Beau ... when you are in the trenches, son, they are all your friends—it is a brotherhood."

Robert noticed the tears in Beau's eyes. "You mentioned you lost an eye in the war, any other injuries?" Robert was enthralled that he was sitting with a veteran and was able to ask him questions.

"Actually, I was wounded twice. Took a bullet in the arm in August 1917. We'd spent the summer in intensive training, learning all kinds of new stuff about fire and movement before our attack on Hill 70. That's where I was wounded." Beau rolled up his sleeve. "See, still have the scar."

Robert squinted, trying to focus in on the scar that was hidden amongst a roadmap of wrinkles. He could not imagine what it would be like to get shot. "When did you lose your eye?"

"August 1918. The 20th was on the move; we'd been given orders, and there was a cloak of secrecy as to where we were actually going. Eventually, we discovered we were to be part of a counter-attack near Amiens. The Battle of Amiens was the turning point; I read that a German commander, in his memoirs, called August 8th 'the black day of the German Army.' Later in the month, our battalion met with more success at Arras, but there was a massive loss of life throughout the ranks.

"I was sent to England to recover but in December the army sent me home. I couldn't shake the depression from the loss of my eye, but it was good to be on home soil again."

"When did your brother return home?"

"The 19th and 20th Battalions arrived in Toronto on May 24th, 1919 … that's when Bob came home. They held an official reception in Varsity Stadium; there was no police force able to hold back the friends and families of these men. It sure was good to see my brother."

"Did you ever get a medal?"

Beau smiled. "Yeah. Soldiers always receive a medal when they get wounded. I got two. My daughter, Donna, has them in her safe deposit box."

A red Honda pulled up in the parking lot, and a lady got out. Robert could tell by seeing her she was Beau's daughter.

"Dad, I'm so sorry I'm late," she said, rushing up to their table. "The doctor was running behind." She extended her hand to Robert. "I can't thank you enough for staying with my dad. I've tried to convince him to get a cellphone for instances like this but he won't have anything to do with them."

"Waste of money at my age, girl." Beau turned to Robert, "Been a pleasure, son."

Robert watched the two leave. He was grateful for the time he had just spent with Beau. He also had gained a whole new outlook on war. He headed back to school and went straight to the library where he searched for information on the 20th Battalion. He learned it had won a total of 18 battle honours and 398 decorations and awards, including two Victoria Crosses. He also learned that during the entire war, the enemy had never driven the 20th from its trenches, nor did any part of it ever flee from the battlefield.

Robert read that over 60,000 Canadian men died in the first World War, one out of every eleven who served. A tear trickled down his cheek. He picked up a pen and began to write.

Beau opened the envelope. A tearstained paper fell out...

Dear Beau: Thank you for our moments; I have written a poem and dedicated it to you and your friends. Hope to see you again. Robert

Sons of Time
Yesterday's sons lie in wait
Reaching skeletal fingers
Sombrely warning
Today's sons
Of the un-glory of war

Yesterday's sons
Have discovered the true meaning
Of glory
As their bones meld together
With their enemies'

Yesterday's sons
Clung to the hope that their sacrifice
Would teach their sons and grandsons
A new meaning to life

Today's son is still fascinated
And manipulated
By the insane warmongers
Who never fight on the battlefront
Themselves

Today's sons tread willingly
Over the old bones
Arrogant that they will return
To their family and friends
Untouched

Madness is the aura of war
Fear feeds the minds
Greed feeds the leaders
Sadness saturates the hearts
Of the mothers
Of yesterday
Of today

Yesterday—gone
Today—going
Tomorrow—questionable

Beau set the poem on his lap. Tears filled his eyes. There was hope; the young man had understood. Beau bowed his head and thanked God for his moments with Robert and prayed that today's youth would never have to see, or live through, what he and his comrades had endured in the first World.

Friends

David and Cameron had been friends since grade school. Even after, while attending different universities, they had maintained contact. Now that they were both married with families, they still got together every couple weeks for a squash game and a drink.

"What's wrong, Cam?" David sensed his friend was troubled.

Cameron hesitated before answering. "Joshua has been having problems with some kids at school. They tease him just so they can watch him lose his temper, then they laugh and goad him on even more. He walloped a boy named Kevin yesterday, gave him a bloody nose. In my opinion, the boy deserved it!" Cameron took a sip of his drink.

"Chip off the old block?" David's eyebrows rose questioningly.

"You might say that; however, Joshua doesn't have a good friend like I had at his age."

"He'll grow out of the tantrums," David offered a ray of hope. "You did."

"Yeah, but it took me until grade seven before I learned to curb my temper; by then, I was labelled. Remember the time on the bus?"

"Oh yeah."

"I hadn't been in trouble for a while because I just started avoiding everyone. After grade six, I spent the whole summer in counselling, and I was determined not to 'lose it' anymore. Everything was going great until Sam Wilson began teasing me on the bus." Cameron's eyes misted over. "He was a real bully; always picking on someone. He just wouldn't stop hammering those words at me..."

David cut in: "I remember him telling you that the reason your parents sent you to camp for the whole summer was that they couldn't stand being around you. I remember that you kept warning him to stop or you would let him have it!"

"You usually didn't take the bus, but I guess your mom was late that day or something, so you thought you better get on," Cameron mentioned.

"And when I stepped on the bus, Sam was chanting that your parents didn't love you, and your face was beet red, but you kept warning him to stop..."

"I remember everyone laughing at me. I think the bus driver or on-duty teacher could have stopped what was about to happen if they'd been paying better attention." Cameron sounded bitter.

"If I remember correctly, Sam got the other guy going too ... what was his name?"

"Mike."

"Yeah, Mike. He started cackling too about your parents not loving you. I could tell you'd had enough, and I was just about ready to tell them to lay off when you up and stuck your fist in Sam's mouth!" David laughed. "I never heard Sam shut up so quickly!"

"Sure, we can laugh now, but all of a sudden the sleepy bus driver woke up and all she saw was me hitting Sam," Cameron stated. "I was hauled off the bus and sent straight to the principal's office. I remember wondering who would believe the 'temper tantrum kid.'"

"I was so upset, I followed you. That's when I saw my mom, and when she came up to me, she knew something was wrong. I told her what happened, and she stood there with her hands on her hips, asking me what I was going to do about helping my friend."

"Your mom was really nice," Cameron said.

"She sure had an inclination for doing what was right; I think she was bullied too in school, from the bits and pieces she mentioned about her school days," David added. "I got to the office just as Mr. Young was giving you the what for. I was surprised when he allowed me to speak on your behalf."

"Me too, and it was good to see Sam and Mike hauled into the office for a lecture about picking on others."

"It ended pretty well," Cameron said as he finished his drink.

"Yep. You and I have never looked back."

"Been good friends all these years."

"The best."

The two men stared at each other for a few moments of awkward silence before David spoke. "Joshua will be okay; he's got you for a dad to help him through this. I'll even bet you that there is someone out there who will stand up for him too, and a few years from now they will be sitting somewhere, like us now, best of friends, talking and laughing about old times."

Cameron was thoughtful as he spoke: "Do you think the cycle of bullying will ever be broken?"

"Probably not, I think there will always be bullies; we just need to teach our kids how to handle them," David replied.

"Yeah, I guess it's all in the handling of these guys," Cameron smiled. "You paying tonight?"

"Your turn, isn't it?"

"Nope. I got it last time…"

"Didn't…"

"Did to…"

The friends laughed and walked to the register. Each paid their own bill.

"You take care of that boy of yours," David called out as he got in his car.

"Thanks, old friend … aren't you glad you have girls?" Cameron returned.

David just smiled as he remembered what had happened to his Emily last week. "Sure, girls are great." He waved goodbye, then drove home to deal with Emily's predicament.

Frank

Dedicated to World War II Veterans

Rose had been assigned to the Veteran's ward in the nursing home. Her co-worker, Julie, told her about one of the WWII vets who dreamt out loud in German and played bagpipe music all day long. It didn't take long to find out who Julie had been talking about. The bagpipe music was a dead giveaway.

"Good morning, sir," she cheerily entered his room. "I am going to be your nurse today."

"Only today?" There was a devilish twinkle in his eyes. "Has my reputation preceded me?"

"Not at all, sir."

"Name's Frank. Didn't you read my chart?"

"I haven't picked it up yet."

"Then why are you here?"

"I heard the bagpipes."

"Hmmmmm…" A coughing spell shook Frank's body. Rose rushed to check the oxygen tubes.

His hand brushed her aside. "I got them."

"Well, I must get my rounds started." She paused at the door, studying the man in the wheelchair. "Would you mind if I came in after work and visited with you? Maybe you could tell me some old war stories? My great-grandfather fought in the first World War, but he never talked about it much…"

"Most of us don't like to talk about those times." Frank coughed again. "But, it would be nice if you visited; I might have a story or two. Maybe, if I tell someone, my nightmares will stop!"

Rose spent the next few weeks visiting Frank after her shift finished. He had allowed her to tape his stories. "Do what you want with them," he had said, his words gurgling from his chest as another coughing fit struck him.

One morning, she went early for her shift, thinking to surprise Frank with a new CD of bagpipe music. His room was empty. She ran to the nurses' station. "Where's Frank?"

"He had a heart attack last night; we tried to reach you…"

"Heart attacks are nothin' compared to what I endured in the war," Frank had told her one day when she'd pointed out his history of heart problems. "Why I remember the day I was almost killed while lying in a hospital bed … we'd been stationed in Holland and had dug deep into the trenches. Good place to dive when the shooting starts … well, the Germans used to shoot these spotter lights up into the air at night, so they could get a spec on our location. We learned how to freeze up pretty quickly, camouflage ourselves right into the landscape. Wasn't hard; most of us were already scared stiff!

"I was a 'bren gunner', and I remember the day I had this German officer and two young soldiers right in my line of fire and I couldn't pull the trigger—those boys were my age—if'n we'd met during different times, we'd most likely have ended up in a pub for a drink!

"Talk today of friendly fire … the German artillery, while firing at us, caught some of their own in the crossfire, killing the lads and wounding the officer. I was hit too, in my belt clip … lost the feeling in my legs. The guys hoisted me onto the hood of a vehicle to get me out of there and on the way we picked up the German officer. We ended up in the same hospital; he was just a man—like me.

"I was in a bed by a huge window. Artillery fire was always rattling the panes, but this one particular day it seemed closer than usual. Instinctively, I pulled the pillow over my head; good I did 'cause the window got hit. When the nurses came to my rescue, there was a giant shard of glass buried in my pillow. Better than in me, I guess."

Rose pictured Frank's smile and the tears hanging from the corners of his tired eyes.

"They hit a school that day, too ... the children's cries as they were brought into the hospital have haunted me all my life."

Rose asked if she could leave to go and see Frank in the hospital.

"Sure," Julie said; "I'll cover for you."

It was a short visit; Rose left in tears. She couldn't bear to see Frank hooked-up to a bunch of machines. She called Julie and asked if she could call someone in to cover her shift. Once at home, Rose made a cup of tea, sat down and turned on the tape recorder...

"I was 18 when I joined—full of dreams, just like all the other boys. The Depression had been tough on us, and a lot of us saw the army as a way to see the world. We sure had our dreams shattered pretty quickly! Young people don't realize just how horrific war is; leaves a man scarred with misery.

"Did my two months of basic training at Camp Borden; I was one of the first young ones in the Underage Company in Meaford. From there, I went to Toronto for advanced training. I remember running through a house filled with tear gas; I had to put an arm across my face to cover my nose, keep my head down, and shut my eyes— no masks.

"The tunnelling really got to me ... claustrophobic, I guess ... then someone would shoot in mustard gas ... couldn't wipe that stuff off ... had to pinch it off...

"Well, finally, we were ready to go. We were all anxious to get over there and fight 'the enemy'! I was in the Royal Regiment of Canada, and we shipped out on the Aquatania, headed for Aldershot, England. Ship had to zigzag to avoid being hit by the enemy subs."

Rose remembered the grin on Frank's face as he relayed the next part of his story...

"We slept in rope hammocks, one on top of the other. The guy under me was a bit of a joker, cut the ropes on my hammock. Well, he suffered more than me, cause I refused to move.

"From England, our regiment was sent to Neopold, Belgium. Eventually, we ended up in the Netherlands, and then Germany. I remember the day I found Maggie—that's what I called her—just as we were crossing over into Germany. She was a Heinz 57 and ugly as they come, but when she gave me kisses all over my hands and face and wagged that stub of a tail, I couldn't leave her behind—wish I had."

The taped played on. Rose was picturing Frank's trembling lips and tear-streaked cheeks as he told her his friends had drowned Maggie. She started to cry as she listened to how he described Maggie's pleading eyes from under the water, and how she had desperately tried to paddle her way out of a watery grave. She heard the anger in his voice as he shouted: "We can't have the mutt giving away our location!"

"But there was a time I had to kill a dog, too. We were holed up in a barn, and this big Shepard managed to sneak in the door; went straight for Larry. I just reacted when I saw the bared teeth reaching for my friend's throat. Didn't take long to snap the dog's neck..."

Rose listened on. Sometimes Frank lapsed into German, which he had learned after the war when he became part of the occupational forces in Germany. "Learned it from the kids who were always asking us for gum and candy—and from the young German girls," Frank added with a sheepish grin.

She cringed when he told her about Fred and George—"Fred's head was blown clear off, right in front of me; George was shot when he approached what he thought was a door. It was a tank ... body parts were everywhere ... nothin' left but his feet stickin' out of his boots. We were supposed to pick up whatever parts we could find, wrap them in a blanket and tie the four corners. I couldn't do it. War is so hideous." Frank had stuttered like a baby while telling that story.

Rose turned off the tape. She decided to pay Frank another visit. There was one story he hadn't told her yet. When she walked into his room, a shadow of a smile crossed his face. She felt a sense of relief to see him awake.

"Hi Frank; how goes it?"

"Goin'; almost gone."

"You mentioned a special lighter to me once..."

"Ah, my lighter," he sighed. "My father gave it to me the Christmas before I enlisted; had my name engraved on it. Can't remember exactly where I lost it—maybe, one of the boats, or a trench somewhere. One day, while in a butcher shop here in Hamilton, a customer heard the butcher call my father by his last name. The man asked my father if he had a son named Frank. His son had found a lighter with my name inscribed on it on a battlefield somewhere in Europe. I let my dad give it to one of his Legion buddies who collected old lighters, but you know, I kinda think I'd like to get it back … I could pass it on to my grandson. Any ideas?"

Rose wiped Frank's sweaty brow. "Do you remember the man's name?"

"John Kindricks … belonged to the Branch 80 Legion."

"I'll see what I can do."

Back in her apartment, Rose listened to the rest of the tape. While in Germany, after the war, Frank had become a batman, a soldier who looked after an officer's garments. He would get the German girls to help him out, giving them blankets in return, which they could make skirts and coats out of. He also used to make extra money by sewing and fixing the guys' jackets.

Frank had returned home on the ship Isle de France, in June of 1946. He was still wearing a kilt, his uniform from having been part of the Queen's Own Regiment. Frank's laughter rolled out of the tape: "You really don't wear anything under the kilt—not allowed. Our regiment leader would lift our kilts up with the edge of his sword to check!"

Frank's sister had met him at the train, bringing her friend, Betty, with her. Frank was as taken with Betty as she appeared to be with his kilt! They were married two years later, in October 1948.

Rose shut the tape off and got out the phonebook. "Hello, Branch 80 Legion."

"Hi, I'm trying to locate a gentleman by the name of John Kindricks…

Frank sensed Rose's presence. "Hey girl, what's up?"

"I have something for you, Frank," Rose smiled indulgently.

His smile was weak. "Well, give it up, girl."

Rose reached into her pocket and then pressed something small into Frank's hand. It felt cool and comforting as he closed his fingers around it. His words staggered with emotion: "Thank you," was all he could manage to get out as tears rolled down his cheeks.

But this time, they were tears of happiness.

Blind Justice

Karen groped around in the room. Someone had moved her furniture—why? She moved further into the space, heading for her kitchen. Damn! Where did this wall come from?

A rustling sound permeated the silence. Karen's head turned to the left, towards where her bedroom should be. She reached out and touched the wall; it would guide her.

"Who's there?" she called out nervously.

Something was rubbing around her legs, something soft. She reached down and her fingertips dug into feline fur. Karen didn't have a cat!

Karen heard the rain start as it began pummelling against the windows. A louder, tapping sound joined the raindrops. What could be making that noise? She didn't have any trees close to her windows.

She continued to follow the wall; her heart was thumping on overdrive. A doorway opened to her probing fingers. She stepped inside. Cold ceramic tiles greeted her socked feet. This was not her bedroom!

What was that smell? Such an overpowering stench. As Karen dared further into what seemed to be the bathroom, her ears picked up a dripping sound. She stepped gingerly forward; her feet collided with something damp.

Karen bent down, and her fingers touched what seemed to be a wet towel, but it wasn't just water. It felt sticky! She touched her finger to her tongue. Blood?

The dripping … the tapping … the rubbing feline … the floor … the changes … Karen continued moving forward, caution thrown aside. Her toes touched the edge of the bathtub. It was solid, unlike her old-fashioned, claw-foot tub. The dripping sound was very loud now. Karen reached to where she assumed a faucet would be. Her hand brushed across something that reminded her of bloody, matted hair—like hers had been on the day a bullet had sunk into her skull. The day she'd lost her sight.

Karen began to back away from what she suspected may be in the tub. The feline let out a yowl as she tripped over it. She was falling on the slippery floor … down … down … no more sound…

"Do you think she did it?" a voice punctured Karen's groggy awakening.

"Her prints are all over the apartment, on the water faucet, too … looks like she smashed his head against that pretty hard … guy bled out in the water."

"Yeah, I don't understand why she left the water dripping though."

Who were these people? A two-way radio crackled. Then a husky voice—one she recognized—Captain Johnston. "Sergeant Mallon, what's the status there?"

"Well, not a wonder the perp didn't come out of his apartment—he's dead! I'd say he's been floatin' in the tub for at least a couple days. Found Karen here … think she might have done it."

"You're kidding, I hope."

"Well Captain, she does have the training, and even if she is blind, she might have pulled this off if she caught him by surprise."

Karen's heart began to race. What were these guys talking about? Who was dead? Why was he being referred to as a perp? Why did they think she killed him?

"Well, Sam Malloney, you finally got what was coming to you, eh?" a new voice commented.

Fear raced through Karen's waking body. Sam Malloney—the guy who had shot her. The big drug-lord—the man she and the team had spent a whole year staking out, waiting for him to slip up. The man she had wished a thousand times she could kill.

Someone was touching her shoulder. "Karen, we have to take you in for questioning."

Karen recognized the voice. James. He'd been on a stakeout with her ... he'd been at the hospital with her ... he'd heard her say how she wanted Malloney dead.

"James?" Karen reached out and touched the face that was close to her. It felt like he hadn't shaved for a week.

James leaned in closer. Karen smelled the cigarette smoke on his breath. "Don't say anything, Karen. I won't give you up. Did a good job though ... Malloney's had this coming for a long time!"

"I didn't do this!" Karen protested. She pushed herself up to a sitting position. James hooked his arm around her and helped her to stand. "I won't cuff you Karen, but I do have to read you your rights...you have the right to..."

"No," Karen groaned.

"Remain silent, you have the right to..."

"No!" she yelled, pulling away and bumping into the doorway. "I didn't do this!"

"Calm down," James ordered.

Karen felt nausea rising in her throat; she knew she was going to pass out again.

"Cuff her, James," the voice who had been referred to as Sergeant Mallon commanded; "can't take a chance on her escaping."

It was at that point she remembered—as Mallon passed by. She recognized his scent—just like Malloney's. A dirty cop ... Mallon ... Malloney ... what was the connection ... oh God ... I couldn't have ... down ... down ... doomed ... dark. Silence. I shouldn't have ... he deserved it though ... and it had been so easy ... he had slipped.

No jury would convict a blind woman...

Figuring it Out

Thanksgiving was just around the corner and Carl didn't have a whole lot to be thankful for. How could his mom be so cheerful; didn't she understand his pain? What about her own suffering? It had all begun in February...

He and his best friend, Don, had decided to take a few days off and go skiing. Don had always been a daredevil. "I want to go off the main trails today; I saw some interesting ones from where we skied yesterday."

Carl closed his eyes. He heard the siren as it had sounded when the avalanche had surged down the mountain. He inhaled sharply as he relived the agony when the rescue team told him they had found Don. A raspy choke gurgled in his throat as he envisioned the funeral.

That was February, and things just kept getting worse...

In March, his dad had an accident at work. A couple of fellows were arguing beside a skid piled high with heavy boxes. As he approached, one of the men pushed the other into the boxes.

They had crashed down on his dad. By the time the boxes were removed, his dad was barely breathing. He had been rushed to the hospital and put on life support.

The doctors had informed Carl and his mom of the extensive damage, saying he would be totally dependent on care—if he came out of his coma.

"What you are saying," Carl had screamed, "is my father is a vegetable! So why did you hook him up to all these bloody machines?"

"Carl," his mom had said, "don't be so harsh; there's always hope."

"Hope? Don't be naïve, Mom!" Carl had shouted before he stormed out.

Carl refused to go with his mom to the hospital. She went faithfully every day. She would call and beg him to go with her; he would just hang up the phone. The day arrived when his mom had decided to let the doctors pull the life support. There was no hope of recovery. Carl had refused to be there. His mom told him his dad had smiled and died peacefully.

Mick, Carl's brother, who was doing a tour of duty in Afghanistan, had been flown home for the funeral. Mick comforted their mom; Carl was too self-absorbed to see beyond his own grief.

"Take care of mom," Mick had said. "Dad was her life."

"Sure, Mick."

"I mean it; snap out of whatever this mood is that you are in and look after mom. If I didn't have to go back right now, I wouldn't." That was the last time Carl saw his brother alive. Two months later, Mick was killed in a roadside bombing.

Carl was crushed. He took the month of June off work and locked himself in his apartment. His mom called every day but he never picked up the phone. His girlfriend, Alicia, had pleaded to him to get it together. After weeks of trying, she had packed her bags and left.

Carl should have returned to work on July 2nd, but the night before he had polished off a bottle of scotch. As a result, he had overslept. When he called in to explain, his manager had told him not to bother coming in. "Get it together, man; you're no good to us like this. Customers don't care about your problems, and we pay you to look after theirs!"

Two weeks later, Carl had received his termination notice. He began throwing things around his apartment. His mom had called; this time he picked up: "What do you want, Mom?" his voice had been harsh.

"I need you, Carl," she had pleaded.

"You don't need me, Mom; I got nothin' to give you." He hadn't even asked her why she needed him.

August blurred into September. His landlord had had numerous complaints about Carl's behaviour. "You've got to settle down, Carl..."

"I pay my rent, don't I?" Carl had yelled belligerently.

"Yes, but..."

Carl had slammed the door. The next day he had received an eviction notice. Carl had opened another bottle of scotch and then called his mom and told her he needed a place to stay. "Just until I get on my feet," he had said.

Carl had made himself comfortable, doing as he pleased, taking no notice of his mom's sadness. He was too absorbed in self-pity. The week before Thanksgiving, his mom had mentioned that she had invited a few friends for Thanksgiving dinner and that she would appreciate his help. He had questioned her sanity at celebrating a holiday so soon after the deaths of her husband and son. Tearfully, she had told him that she still had a lot to be thankful for; there were many people worse off than she was. Carl had stormed out the door.

Two days later when he returned, the house was decorated for Thanksgiving and smelled of pumpkin delights.

"Hello, Carl," his mom had greeted him as he had staggered into the kitchen. "Are you feeling okay, you're so pale."

"I'm fine," he had replied curtly.

His mom had cut him a piece of pumpkin pie. "Here, this will make you feel better."

"I doubt it," he had said, but he had eaten the pie anyway.

"Carl! The guests are arriving; could you give me a hand to put the food out?"

All morning Carl's nostrils had been teased by the savoury aroma of his mom's cooking. Only now he remembered that she had asked him to help, but he had opened his bottle instead. Carl stumbled to the bathroom and splashed water on his face. When he gazed into the mirror, he had no idea who was looking back at him!

The once dark, mischievous eyes were now dismal, saturated with pain. Black circles cocooned the sunken sockets. His cheeks caved in and his mouth curled downward, barely visible in a scruffy beard. His hair was long and unkempt. He looked like a homeless man.

"Carl, all the guests are here!"

"Be down in a sec, Mom."

When Carl walked into the dining room, there was not one person that he knew sitting at the table. There was a young man in a wheelchair; a little girl with a bald head. Beside the girl was a haggard looking woman, who fussed continuously over the child. At the end of the table was an elderly man with a humped back; beside him, a lady with a portable oxygen tank. There was a teenager, barely 15, whose belly was swollen with child. Beside her was a young boy; in place of his arms were rounded stubs of flesh. The boy smiled at Carl.

The little girl looked up at him. "You must be Carl; it's about time you joined us. Your mom wouldn't start without you!"

His mom entered the room with a platter laden with turkey and vegetables. "Help yer mother, boy!" the old man ordered.

"Who do you think you are, ordering me? This is my home..." Carl began.

Carl's mom set the platter down. "No, Carl, this is my home, and these are my guests. You will treat them with respect."

Her harsh tone startled him. As Carl gazed into her eyes, he saw her naked pain. Her hands trembled. He hung his head as he reached for the platter and began to serve the guests. The only sound in the room was the clinking of utensils and the hissing sound of the lady's oxygen tank. Carl's mom brought out more bowls of food and passed them around.

Once everyone's plates were filled, she sat down and reached out her hands. Everyone did the same until the circle was complete. "I want everyone to say at least one thing they are thankful for before we begin this Thanksgiving meal; I will start. I am thankful for my son and all my new friends. Even though this year has been challenging, having buried my husband and my oldest son, I still have Carl, and I have had the good fortune of meeting all of you who have each specially touched my life."

"I am thankful that Lydia talked to the doctors and I have been given the okay to have my dream trip to the Rocky Mountains," the little girl said.

Her mother, in a barely audible whisper: "I am thankful that I will have at least six more wonderful months with my daughter."

"I am thankful my baby isn't damaged, even though I was heavy into drugs and alcohol. Thank you, Lydia, for sticking by me and keeping me strong enough to walk away from that world."

Carl looked at his mom. She had a serene smile on her lips.

"I am thankful for the outings that Lydia takes me on. I have no family or anyone else who cares. Without her, I would still be a shut-in." The young man in the wheelchair looked adoringly at Carl's mom.

The little boy giggled. "I am thankful for all the stories Lydia reads to me; she is so funny the way she acts out the characters in different voices. That is how my mom and dad used to read me stories before they died."

"I am thankful for the wonderful 60 years I have had with my Sarah, despite all our hardships. I am thankful for the wonder of having held my son in my arms, even if it was only for a few hours," the old man choked.

His wife patted his hand. "I am thankful for this wonderful man who has been unwavering in his love for me; standing by me through all my years of illness. We are thankful for Lydia, who has been a blessing in our lonely lives."

There was a moment of silence. Carl looked up. Everyone was staring at him. "Well, boy, what are you thankful for?" the old man prodded.

Carl cleared the emotion from his throat. He fixed his eyes on his mom. "I am thankful for my mom and this Thanksgiving Day that she has given me."

"Amen!" the little girl shouted. "Let's eat."

Malcolm

Malcolm stared longingly at the bright lights. He watched with envy as people came and went from the building. He noticed the ones with smiles; he failed to see the ones walking with lifeless steps. He cursed the establishment for having banned him from the premises for … well, he couldn't remember for how long.

He held a wrinkled paper bag to his lips, lowered it, and then flicked his tongue out to catch a stray drop. It escaped into his scraggly whiskers. "There was a day when you all smiled when I came through your doors!" Malcolm shouted, raising his fist. He quickened his pace. It would be dark soon and the chill November winds were biting through his ragged coat.

Malcolm took one last glance at the casino lights. As he turned, his foot slipped off the sidewalk and he tumbled onto the street. The last thing he heard was the screech of tires.

The bright light was penetrating his eyes; it hurt like hell! He was laying on something soft. There were strange people all around him. "Do you know this man?" a voice asked.

"I am not sure; there is something familiar about him." Malcolm turned his eyes to the voice. There was a recognizable tone to it. He tried to focus.

"He didn't have any I.D. on him," a female voice mentioned. "What is your name, sir?"

"He's too drunk to know what you are saying," a different female voice alleged.

"Well, he was just hit by a car…"

"I was the one who had to change him into hospital garb when he arrived; trust me, Rose; he's drunk!"

Malcolm felt a warm hand on his forehead, and the gentler voice spoke again. "What is your name?"

"Malcolm, name's Malcolm Turin."

The man who had brought Malcolm into the hospital gasped. The doctor looked at him. "So you do know him?"

"I think so … I knew a Malcolm Turin once, years ago. We were best friends. We got into a bit of trouble; he went one way, I went the opposite." The man ran his fingers through his hair.

"Well we won't be much longer here," the doctor began; "maybe he'll talk more when we are gone."

Malcolm's blood pressure and pulse were retaken, and then the medical staff left, leaving the man in street clothes alone with Malcolm. He sat down in the chair beside the bed.

"Malcolm Turin, eh … Remember me? … John Mason. We were best friends about ten years ago … we worked at Granton Machine Shop."

Malcolm stirred at the sound of familiar names. He squinted at the man beside him and his memory flickered. "John Mason, eh? Granton Machine Shop … Hell, that was years ago … how many did you say?"

"About ten."

"That long, eh?"

"The last time we saw each other was our court date. You stormed out, cursing the judge, the system, everything you could think of to curse," John said.

Malcolm smiled. "Yeah, I remember now. We used to kick up quite a storm, didn't we? Too bad we got caught."

"I am thankful we did; it turned my life around. I'm married now: beautiful wife, two great kids; house in a new survey; and a great job." John paused, not wanting to ask the next question. "What have you been up to?"

"Fitness training," Malcolm laughed.

"I don't quite understand."

"I walk around all day."

John started to laugh, clueing into what Malcolm meant. "Where do you live?" he dared to ask.

"By the Lorne Bridge."

"On Grand River Ave?"

Malcolm looked away, embarrassed. "No, under the bridge."

"Want a coffee?" John asked.

"Where's my bottle?"

John stood. "I'll get you a coffee."

While John was gone, Malcolm travelled down memory lane. He and John had been heavy into casino gambling. They were young and had thought nothing could touch them. They had won big a couple of times, and then things had headed downhill. There had been loss after loss, and they had borrowed money from some guys with bad reputations. When the loans were due, the money wasn't there, so they concocted a plan to take a few tools from the shop and sell them under the table. That had worked for a while until they were caught! He had not seen John since the court date. After finishing his community service, he had headed back to the casino. Life had not improved much.

John returned with the coffee and they chatted a while. Finally, he looked at his watch and said he had to get going. "Here is my phone number." He placed a business card in Malcolm's hand. "Give me a call when you get out of here, and we'll catch up some more."

"Got some change?"

The Real Mom

Francine's hand rose hesitantly at the door. She lowered it and then re-summoned her courage and knocked. She was just about to leave when the door opened a crack.

"Who is it?" a youthful voice asked.

"My name is Francine; is your mom home?"

"She's sleeping."

"I'll come back later then." Francine felt a flush of relief at not having to face Carla.

"Who's at the door, Kelly?" a woman's voice called.

"Some lady named Francine."

"Tell her to wait, please … actually, let her in and show her to the living room; I'll be right there."

The door opened and Francine was face to face with a girl of about ten. She could tell the child was Carla's daughter, probably the baby Carla had been expecting when she had left.

"Follow me," Kelly said, leading the way. "Mom will be here in a minute." Kelly sat down across from Francine. She was looking at something on the wall behind Francine. "You're her," she exclaimed.

"Who?"

"The one in the picture." Kelly pointed.

Francine turned and looked. She swallowed hard. It was the last school picture she'd had taken while living with Carla and Nick. She had been 12. That was ten years ago but it felt like a lifetime!

"Francine, how are you?" Carla bustled into the room. Her gentle blue eyes and open arms invited Francine for a hug. "Kelly, this is Francine; she used to live with Dad and me before you were born."

"Why doesn't she live with us now?"

"Well," Carla paused; "Francine had her own mom, and she went to live with her."

"Why did she leave her mom in the first place?"

Carla glanced at Francine, who was fidgeting nervously with her purse strap. "Her mom was ill for a very long time; she wasn't able to look after Francine, so your dad and I did for a while."

"How long?"

"Two years."

Kelly was puzzled. "That's a long time; I don't think I could be without you for two years!" She turned to Francine, "Didn't you miss your real mom?"

Francine blushed. Carla stood up. "Kelly, don't you have some chores to do? I'd like to talk a bit with Francine and catch up on what she has been doing since I saw her last." She turned to Francine: "Would you like a drink, honey?"

Francine nodded.

"Tea okay?"

"That would be nice."

Carla finished making the tea and set two cups on the table. "It's good to see you; I think of you often, but you never contacted me after you moved away."

"I have a little girl."

"How lovely; how old is she?"

"She just turned six," Francine smiled. "Her name is Serena; she's my whole life now."

"Do you have a picture of her?"

Francine pulled out her wallet and flipped to the pictures of Serena.

"She's beautiful." Carla paused. "So ... how are things with you?"

Tears welled up in Francine's eyes. "I'm pregnant."

"That will be nice for Serena to have a little brother or sister."

"Yeah, but..." The tears began to flow. "He left me ... said he didn't want another kid ... said I should have known better ... I should have seen the signs ... he never really paid attention to Serena ... maybe because she wasn't his..."

Carla's hand reached instinctively to cover Francine's trembling ones. "You'll be okay. Is your mom still around?"

Francine's laugh gurgled through her tears. "She took off with another man not long after Serena was born ... told me I'd got knocked up and it wasn't her responsibility to bail me out or look after the brat." Francine's breath was ragged as she continued: "You would never have left me, Mom; you would never have made me face that on my own; you would have been there for me. I was a fool to have left you, Mom. I was a fool to have listened to the tales the woman who gave birth to me spun. She promised me things would be better if I came back to her. It was okay at first; I cooked and cleaned while she went out and partied. That kept her happy. Then when I got pregnant and was having a difficult time, I couldn't do all that anymore. The doctor ordered bed rest for the last three months of my pregnancy, and he told her she'd have to look after me. But she didn't. She told the doctor she was; she told everyone else I was lazy!"

"Where was the father?" Carla asked softly.

Francine smirked. "He took off; a pregnant woman, in his eyes, wasn't desirable. He found greener fields to mow!"

Carla poured them another cup of tea. "Where are you living now?"

"Brantford, with my half-sister, Janine."

"How is she doing?" Carla asked. She remembered back to the first time she had met Janine. She had been a quiet girl with sad, dark eyes. She had also been too old for her skin. Things had been done to her that no young girl should ever have to experience.

"Janine has a boy and a girl from the man she'd been living with. I remember telling you, Mom, how he treated her so much better than my daddy had—that he loved her. But, he didn't.

You were the one who told me that a girl's body was sacred to self, and it was our decision when to share it. When I told my sister that, she told me she was happy. She said that the man loved her! One day, Janine caught him going after her little girl and realized it was just young girls he loved; he hadn't been with her for months! Janine called our mother, and, of course, she did no more for Janine than she'd done for me ... 'you make your bed, you lie in it,' I think were our mother's exact words!"

"She did well to get out," Carla stated. There was a quiet silence as the women finished their tea.

Francine stared out the window. "I wish I'd never left you, Mom," she whispered.

Carla's heart melted. She had no idea how much she had actually touched Francine in the two years the girl had been in her home. She remembered the first time Francine had called her "mom" two days after her arrival. She remembered how the young girl had flourished: her self-esteem had grown, her school marks became A's instead of D's, she smiled and laughed; she was being the child she had never been allowed to be.

But then things had changed. Francine had become sullen and argumentative. Carla received phone calls from the teacher regarding inappropriate behaviour. Her school marks began to fall. And then Carla had noticed a strange phone number on the bill. When she called it, Francine's mother had answered.

Carla and Nick had called her social worker in to discuss the situation. Francine admitted she had been in contact with her mother and that she wanted to go back to her. Her mother had filled her head with the idea she would never be good enough to fit in with the foster family, especially now that they were expecting a child of their own. She had told Francine she wanted her back and had promised things would be different.

Carla remembered sitting on the couch, her heart torn apart, as Francine stood firm on her decision. And the two-year limit was up, so the CAS had to either keep her as a permanent ward of the province or send her back to one of her birth parents!

Francine looked so fragile—so vulnerable. Carla smiled. "If you remember, I told you my door would always be open to you."

"I remember, Mom."

"Welcome home."

Sahar

The letter dropped to the floor. Rowan's hands shook. She had actually had no idea just how much pain war caused until this past summer when she had volunteered for the medical corps in Kabul, Afghanistan. Newspapers and newscasts hadn't sufficiently related to her the realities she witnessed there. And now, her brother's letter drove another nail into her fragile frame. Colin wrote that her friend, Sahar, had been killed in a roadside bombing while on her way to a village medical outreach project.

Rowan took out her diary and flipped to the first page...

Saturday, May 24: I have arrived in Kabul today. I am excited about this adventure and anxious to see Colin, who has been in Afghanistan for six months. I hope to get out to his base tomorrow because I start at the hospital on Monday. I am living in a private home which is situated in a walled compound near many of the Embassy buildings. I am happy that I have full bathroom facilities.

Monday, May 26: I arrived at the Kabul hospital this morning and met Sahar. She told me how thrilled her family was that she was studying to be a nurse. She told me there was a great need in her country for well-trained medical staff. I was surprised at Sahar's command of the English language as she showed me around the hospital.

Friday, May 30: It has been a busy week. My hours are long, but my eyes are being opened wide to the tragedies in this country. Today I met Hassan. He is studying to be a doctor. He told me that in 2003, his first year of internship, the hospital had only just obtained some of the much needed medical equipment. I was astounded that things I took for granted, like ultrasound machines and incubators, had been non-existent in the hospital in 2002, leaving many women, especially those with a high-risk pregnancy, with limited help.

Monday, June 2: Sahar took me out after work today to show me the reality in the lives of some women living in her country. I felt confined in the burqa Sahar gave me, but she insisted we wear them, saying that way we would not be bothered while walking on the street. She took me to a modern shopping mall in the downtown area. I thought I was walking through a mall in downtown Toronto. Western-influenced clothing stores sported posters of young people dressed in jeans and T-shirts. There was even one poster, at the entrance of a female clothing shop, of a mini-skirt clad woman hugging a man. Jewellery stores are everywhere, and modern music blares from the mall speakers.

Before leaving the mall, we had a supper of lamb kebab and rice, and Bichak, which are small turnovers filled with potato and herbs. I ordered Gosh Feel, thin pastries covered in powdered sugar and ground pistachios, for dessert. I will write more tomorrow; it has been a long night, physically and mentally...

Tuesday, June 3: I am shaken by the news that another Canadian soldier has been killed by direct fire when a joint Afghan-Canadian security patrol came under fire from insurgents in the Panjwayi District. I prayed it was not Colin ... it wasn't.

Last night was eye-opening for me. After leaving the mall, Sahar took me along some streets where women in burqas were begging. "These are the hidden faces of our country," she told me. "There are around two million war widows, and it is so easy for people to forget about their plight with such modern malls, as we just came from, opening everywhere."

Sahar then took me to meet her friend, Zenab, who lives with her mother, Houda, in one of many abandoned buildings in an old section of the city. Houda is a widow. She told me, over a cup of watery tea, how she is reduced to begging on the street and makes about 50 afghanis a day, barely enough for two pieces of bread. She has no relatives to take her in or offer any kind of financial support.

Zenab is 17. She is bitter at the government for all its empty promises. She told me she cannot afford the supplies needed to be able to attend school. Her mother barely makes £125 a year. Zenab cried when she told me nothing has really changed for her family in the new Afghanistan. It actually worsened after her father was killed. Houda hung her head as she talked of the abuse and harassment she is accosted with on the streets; but said she is grateful for the burqa, which hides her identity, allowing her some dignity.

Saturday, June 7: I am troubled by Houda's story, and by what I am seeing. Sahar and I spent last night at a restaurant talking. She talked about the suicide rate among Afghan widows, many of whom saw that as their only escape from misery. She showed me an article which revealed that many Afghani women are victims of mental and sexual violence and that their life span is 20 years less than women living in other parts of the world. Many women and girls have resorted to prostitution, and the numbers will continue to rise as they try to escape poverty unless something drastic is done! Sahar said that even their fellow women discriminate because most Afghan men do not want to marry someone previously married, and with children. They think it an insult to their honour—even if the woman is a widow!

Wednesday, July 9: It has been a while since my last entry. I had the opportunity to travel to a village medical outreach project. I cannot believe the lack of healthcare in Kandahar Province, but Hassan, who was also on the trip, told me that because of security problems, many agencies are hesitant to invest time or money. We treated people with dehydration, malnutrition, muscular-skeletal issues, upper respiratory infections, cancer and congenital deformities—just to mention a few. The people were so grateful, and my heart is touched, especially by the children whose smiles are worth more than a million words.

Sahar is happy I am back. We celebrated by going to the Bahg-e Babur Gardens, which is filled with beautiful roses. She said it had been destroyed in the war but the Aga Khan Foundation and the Germans restored it. We enjoyed a dish of ice cream and then listened to some traditional Afghan music at the French Institute. It is beautiful to see Westerners and Afghanis gathered in one place, even though there was a suicide bombing at the Indian Embassy just two days ago.

Another Canadian soldier has been killed. An explosive device detonated near a dismounted security patrol in the Panjwayi District. I continue to pray for my brother's safety, and for that of all soldiers and their families, both foreign and Afghani.

Monday, July 21: I received a letter from Colin telling me about his patrol's excursion into Kandahar City. Kids were throwing rocks at their vehicles, and his troop was assigned to go there to get them to stop. By the time they left, the children had won their hearts. They are so innocent, Colin wrote; I guess, for them, it is just like us throwing snowballs at cars.

Friday, August 1: Sahar took me to meet her friend, Salman, who owns a book store in Kabul. He told me he had been imprisoned numerous times because of the forbidden books he sold. He is passionate about literature and gave me a book of poetry. He asked me if I had thought about staying on in Kabul, as a nurse. I told him that I honestly didn't know if I could.

Saturday, August 9: Another Canadian soldier has died. I also received a letter from my mother. She is worried and wants me to return home. I know she would like Colin to come home too, but that is not in our hands. I am anxious for my mother; I am fearful for the friends I have made here in Kabul.

Thursday, August 21: Three more of our soldiers were killed in the Zharey District when their vehicle was struck by an explosive device. I cannot help but worry that one of them is Colin; I pray for peace, and for the wives and children at home who have lost a loved one.

I will be returning to Canada soon. My classes begin on September 8th. I have prolonged my stay here in Kabul to the 5th. Sahar and I have become like sisters. We both dread our upcoming parting.

Thursday, September 4: I am preparing to leave tomorrow. Tragedy struck our Canadian forces yet again. Three soldiers were killed and five injured when their armoured vehicle was attacked in the Zharey District. I won't be able to see my brother; he is out on patrol. Sahar has invited me to have supper with her family tonight. I cannot bear to leave her.

Hassan has wished me well and said he hoped I would return. I could be one of his surgical nurses, he suggested. We laughed despite the tears in our eyes.

Friday, September 5: I am on the plane. My pen is as empty of ink as my heart is of joy. Sahar embraced me at the airport. She smiled and told me that if I returned, we would get a place together. She said she would find me a nice Afghani boy to marry—maybe Hassan. We laughed. We would raise our babies together…

Rowan closed the diary. She buried her face in a pillow and let the tears flow … for that which was … for that which never would be.

Rosa and Rosco, Christmas 2008

The snow fell gently as Nadine walked the river trail. Her Grandma Rosa's health was not good. The doctor had told the family she would be lucky to see another six months; the cancerous tumour was too far advanced to operate on. It was now December 20th, and Rosa was still here. Nadine had moved in with her grandma because her mother hadn't been able to handle the caregiving alone.

One day in early December, Grandma Rosa had caught Nadine moping. "I'll still be here for Christmas; don't you worry, child," she had said.

"But, the doctor said…"

"Matters not what he said. What do doctors know anyway?" Rosa had laughed. And then Nadine had laughed. And then Rosa had told her what she wanted for Christmas, and Nadine had promised to make it happened, not thinking that she would have to fulfill that promise. Now, Christmas was only five days away, and it looked like Nadine was going to have to make good on her word.

She saw her favourite bench, brushed it off, sat down and stared out at the frigid waters of the Grand River. She and her grandma had sat on this bench many times. Sometimes, they would bring a picnic lunch, and Nadine would listen to her grandma's stories. She especially loved the ones of Christmas. Of all the holidays, her grandma loved Christmas the most; yet when she told her Christmas stories there always seemed to be a veiled sadness in her eyes. During the past summer, she had confided to Nadine…

"You are old enough now to understand that things sometimes happen in families. It happened on Christmas Day, 40 years ago. My brother walked out of the house, never to be seen or heard from again. The words were out of my cousin's mouth before I could intervene, and once they were said, that was it! My brother stood up and quietly left the room. We all thought he was just going to cool off, but when he didn't return after a couple of hours, I went looking for him. I found this note on his bed ... we were twins, you know..."

Nadine hadn't known her Grandma Rosa even had a brother ... not even her mother had mentioned him.

Dear Rosa: I can take no more accusations, so I have decided to remove myself from the family so as not to embarrass them further. I have actually been planning this for some time, so you needn't worry. Don't try to find me. Take care, my dearest sister, my soul mate, for even though I leave this house, you will be forever in my heart. Love, Roscoe.

"I ran outside," Grandma Rosa had continued on. "Roscoe's footprints were barely visible, and I followed them to the trail, but the wind was swirling the snow and the prints soon disappeared. I returned to the house. Oh, Nadine, my sweet child, my grief turned to anger. Everyone was joking and making fun of Roscoe, saying he had run off to sulk like a baby!"

"What did Roscoe do that was so bad?" Nadine interrupted.

Rosa had hesitated. "He was accused of something terrible, and because of his mental illness, every Tom, Dick, and Harry pronounced him guilty before he even went to trial. It was a trying time for the family. He was eventually cleared, but the stigma was still there. From the start, only I defended him, knowing he couldn't have done such a terrible thing. We being twins and all—I just knew!"

Nadine had chosen not to pursue the question of what Grandma Rosa's brother, Roscoe, had been accused of doing. Nor did she question further about his mental illness. Her grandma would tell her in time if she wanted to.

Nadine stood and headed for home. The snow had already covered her previous tracks. She had a lot to accomplish over the next few days if she was to pull together the perfect Christmas for her grandma.

Sitting down at her computer, Nadine typed in "Roscoe Salino." She was surprised at the number of hits. Two hours later, Nadine stood up and stretched her stiff muscles. She had sent off 36 emails to possible candidates. She headed to the basement where all the old photo albums were. Her mother had judiciously labelled them, and Nadine quickly found the one for Christmas 1968. She began flipping through it, taking notes of how things had been decorated then and who was at the party. The last picture was of her Grandma Rosa sitting beside a young man. They were looking into the mirrors of their souls, and there was such a peaceful look on their faces. Underneath was written, "Rosa & Roscoe, Christmas 1968!" Nadine touched the picture lovingly before closing the book and heading upstairs.

A busy two days passed. There were no answers to any of the emails, but the house was beginning to look like a 1960's Christmas. Rosa told Nadine where the old decorations were and supervised her while she put together a long-forgotten nativity scene. Nadine replaced the artificial tree with a real one. Rosa decorated the bottom branches and instructed how the upper ones should look. They laughed together, and Nadine heard more stories of Christmases past, the ones her grandma had spent with her brother, Roscoe.

Nadine cleaned out the fireplace and purchased some wood from a friend. She hung cedar boughs over the doorways and placed candles on the coffee table. Rosa reminded Nadine of what she would like to eat for Christmas: "Roscoe always preferred a goose," she smiled. Nadine went to the market and returned with the biggest goose she could find, for she was not sure how many of her grandma's cousins would actually show up; the notice was short most had said.

Christmas Eve arrived. There had been no positive replies from any of the e-mails. Nadine's mother, who was away on a short holiday, called and said her flight was delayed and she would not be arriving until 5:30 on Christmas Day. She would take an airport taxi; no need to pick her up.

Light snow was falling on Christmas morning. Nadine helped her grandma into a red dress, similar to the one she had worn in 1968. She wrapped a new red shawl around her grandma's frail shoulders, and then styled her hair into a French-twist and placed a red, silk rose on the right side—just how Rosa had worn her hair in 1968.

By 4:00 the snow was coming down so heavily that Nadine could not even see the houses on the other side of Dufferin Avenue. She started the fireplace. The goose would be done soon. She wrapped the pots of cooked vegetables in a blanket to keep them warm. At 4:30, one of her grandma's cousins called to say they weren't coming. Nadine assumed none of them would come—because of the weather, of course. It was a good excuse.

Rosa started humming. Even though she was in good spirits, Nadine noticed her grandma's face was quite sallow. "Sing with me, Nadine," and Nadine joined in halfway through *Oh Holy Night*. At 5:00, Nadine's mother called and said she was stuck at the Toronto Airport and was going to get a hotel room for the night. The roads were bad. She was sorry.

We may as well eat, Grandma," Nadine suggested.

Rosa smiled. "No, I think I'll wait for Roscoe; he'll be along soon."

Nadine sighed. "I wasn't able to find him, Grandma. I am so sorry."

"He'll be here; we are twins, you know. I feel him close by. You eat if you want, dear; I'll just wait for him."

At 6:00, the doorbell rang. "I wonder which cousin has braved the storm," Nadine said, heading for the door.

"It's Roscoe," Rosa whispered, her face lighting up with joy.

"Probably not, Grandma." Nadine opened the door. A tall, elderly man stood there shivering in the cold December winds.

"Are you Nadine? I hope I am not too late." He smiled. It was her Grandma Rosa's smile.

"Yes, I'm Nadine."

"I am Roscoe; is Rosa here?"

January 2nd was bright and crispy. The funeral was well attended by family, all hoping to catch a glimpse of the long-lost Roscoe; but he was long gone. He had told Nadine he had only come for his sister, Rosa; he wanted nothing to do with the rest of them. Nadine understood after having witnessed their few short days together. Roscoe had held Rosa's hand during her last breaths.

Nadine sat down in her Grandma Rosa's chair. She picked up the photo album marked 1968 and flipped to the last page. There was room enough for one more picture. Nadine placed a new one in; her fingers tracing tenderly over the profiles of two people sitting side by side, gazing lovingly into the mirrors of their souls.

She picked up a pen and wrote underneath the photo: *"Rosa & Roscoe; Christmas 2008."*

A Letter from the Past

Murray put the decorations in the plastic bin and closed the lid. Another Christmas over with and now he could go back to the reality of life. He had put on, as he did every year, the façade for the family, but he swore this was the last time. From now on, he would celebrate the holidays the way he wanted to and the family would just have to deal with it; he was past caring.

Murray sat down at his computer. He looked at the pile of mail that had been there since before Christmas. A pale-blue envelope with a French postage stamp caught his attention. He lifted it to his nose; it smelled musty. He turned it over, looking for a return address. None.

"May as well open it," he muttered. He pulled out a letter; it was dated, December 23, 1958…

My dearest Murray: It is with the heaviest heart that I write this letter to you. I have no valid excuse for leaving without saying goodbye. I have taken that teaching position, which we talked about, and I will be staying with my friend, Adele, who lives in Paris, until I find my own place.

I know it would have been tough for you to have left your family and your career, and I saw how torn you were when we discussed the possibility of both of us going to France. So, I made the decision for you, as cowardly as it was of me.

Your sister, Sandy, mentioned you had something special for me for Christmas. I was afraid if I stayed that I would not be able to go after receiving your gift. I too had something special for you, but feared if I gave it to you … well, I am not quite sure what I feared.

Already it has been three days without you, and my heart is so heavy with the loss of not seeing your face and not having your arms wrapped around me. As I write this letter, I admonish myself for the fool I may be. You are the only man I have ever loved and ever will love.

Adele's address is on the back of my letter. I pray you will find it in your heart to forgive me, and that you will write to me, telling me what a dimwit I am to have left you; for, now that the deed is done, I do not have the courage to undo it.

With all my love, Molly

Murray dropped the letter on the desk. He thought about the emptiness of his life since the day she had left. He thought about what it might have been like had she stayed; about how it could have been had he actually had the courage to leave his job and follow her to France. He could have found a teaching position there; he had been fluent in French.

And then he thought about the hurt and the embarrassment he had suffered, and his heart hardened. He thought about the years of loneliness he had endured because there had never been anyone quite like Molly. Murray had buried himself in his work. Then, he thought of the little red box tucked in the top drawer of his dresser, hidden by his socks. He thought of the number of times he had been going to return it but had not. Because he could not.

Murray picked up the letter and gazed at the address on the back. Why hadn't this letter arrived 50 years ago! Would that have changed anything? Or would his pride, hurt by her having left without a word, have stilled his heart?

He retrieved the little red box and gazed at its content. Then he took out a piece of paper and began to write…

Dear Molly: I just received your letter. I have been keeping something for you; maybe with the anticipation that one day I would see you again. I hope it still fits. I never met anyone else who seemed appropriate for it…

Murray paused. Slowly, he crumpled his letter and threw it into the wastebasket. He held the little red box in his hand for a moment and then snapped it shut. He returned it to its hiding place, along with Molly's letter. Maybe, he would have the courage on another day. Today was not it.

The letter was dated December 23, 2010. It was tucked beside a little red box in a shipping envelope…

Dear Molly: Murray asked me to send this to you. He only received the letter you sent him in 1958 a couple of years ago. He said he wanted to write to you then but didn't have the courage. He never married; you were his only love … Sandy

Molly slid the ring on her finger and touched it to her heart.

Into the Light

I slammed my fist on the arm of my wheelchair. I was tired of being in the hospital. It had been a year and a half. I glared out the window. There was a lot one could see from the top floor of a building.

The twins were playing in their yard. The first time I had seen them, they were in a playpen. They could barely walk around the sides of it. Their mother had laughed as the twins had bumped into each other and fell down. Now, the twins were running around the backyard.

I gazed to the left, at a small apartment building with a rooftop garden. The old lady was watering and pruning her plants. I wondered why she bothered because last fall, just as the plants matured, some neighbourhood youngsters had snuck up to the roof and, what they could not eat, they destroyed. I had watched them. I could identify them for her. Harvest time was almost here; they were lurking again.

My eyes roved to the other side of where the twins lived. What a beautiful sight. I wondered how many years he had been working on that body. He moved with the grace of a big cat; every morning as the sun rose, every evening as the sunset. I ran my fingers down the window pane, tracing the ripples in his arms and legs. Sometimes he would look my way and I would dream of possibilities.

A knock at the door startled me back to reality. No one actually expected me to answer—it was a hospital. They were all just being polite, informing me that they were barging in! One day I would get the courage to holler out, "Just a minute, please." Maybe, today … too late. I grimaced. Aunt Ester walked in.

"Hello, Aunt Ester."

"Hello, dear, how are you today?" She hovered. Her voice always grated on my nerves.

"Same as I was yesterday when you left," I mumbled.

"What was that, dear? Speak up. You know my hearing's bad."

"I'm fine, Aunt Ester." I turned and looked out the window. Aunt Ester began straightening the covers on my bed. I had told her a thousand times that the nurses looked after that; she had told me the same amount of times that nurses were overworked. She should know. She used to be one.

"Would you like me to take you downstairs to the indoor hospital garden, dear?" Aunt Ester asked as she finished fluffing my pillow.

Before I could stop them, the words were out of my mouth. "I'd like you to take me outside today."

After a moment's silence, "But I thought you told the doctor last week that you weren't ready to go out yet."

"I'm ready today." I turned my wheelchair around to face her. "I want to meet my friends."

"Your friends? Well, they all know they have to come and see you here; that things are difficult for you."

"But they don't, so I have made new ones. Come and take a look." I turned back to the window and pointed to the yard where the twins were. "I have been watching them grow; I would like to know their names." I motioned over to the apartment building. "I would like to tell that lady to take care of her garden because there are some boys who will be there soon, and they will destroy it before she gets any benefit from it."

"But dear..."

"No buts, Aunt Ester; I have saved the best till last." I indicated the location where the young man was practicing on his back deck. "Especially do I want to meet him and learn his name, and then tell him mine."

"I see," said Aunt Ester with a smile.

"I have some scarves in my closet there. Please get me two; one for my head, for I see a breeze in the trees, the other, a lighter one, for my face, to protect me from the sun."

"What will the doctor say?"

"Doesn't matter."

Aunt Ester went hesitantly to my closet. When she had me bundled as requested, she grabbed a blanket from the end of my bed and tucked it around my legs. "It's still a bit chilly outside."

We headed out of my room and stopped at the elevator. My heart was beating fast as we passed through the metal doors. My stomach took flight as we descended. I shook with excitement as the doors parted and Aunt Ester pushed me across the lobby, out of the hospital and into the sunlight.

I raised my covered face and reached my hand up to touch the warmth for the first time since the fire, a year and a half ago.

White Roses

A Valentine's Day Story

The single white rose arrived at Sandra's door at 3:00 p.m. on Valentine's Day. There was no card. The delivery boy could not tell her who sent it.

Sandra tipped him and closed the door. She had to get ready for work. She had switched a shift with her friend, Lena, whose boyfriend had planned something special for them. Sandra was not interested in such trivialities; she had her nursing career—that was her love. Maybe someday a man would fit into her life, but not now. She put the rose in a vase and set it on the kitchen table. Sandra had no idea who could have sent it. And, she had not thought to ask the delivery man which florist he worked for.

Her shift was quiet for a Friday night. "I guess everyone is making love tonight, not war," Sandra laughed as she sat down at the nurses' station.

Hilda, the supervisor, chuckled. "Well, for all the years I've been working in Emergency, Valentine's Day has always been fairly quiet." She paused. "When are you going to get someone in your life, girl? You don't want to end up a miserable, old maid like me, do you? When was the last time you had a date?" Hilda's eyes penetrated for an answer.

"I don't have time for men right now. I've worked hard to get my degree, and I'm not finished yet. Actually, I have my sights set on your job, Hilda—when you retire, of course."

"There are days, girl, when I would gladly give you my job!" Hilda's face turned serious. "Don't you think it would be nice to receive flowers from someone special on Valentine's Day—just once?"

Sandra wheeled her chair over to Hilda. "Why Hilda darling, I had no idea you were such a romantic!" She grinned mysteriously. "I did get a flower this afternoon—a white rose."

Hilda's face showed her shock. "From who?"

"Don't know."

"No idea?"

"Nope. No card … just a single white rose."

"Well, the florist should have a record of who ordered it," Hilda pushed on.

"I forgot to ask which florist, and the deliveryman was using his own car."

"Maybe it was him."

"Nope, never seen him before."

An ambulance siren sounded. Sandra and Hilda sprang into action.

Sandra was preparing for work. It had been 30 years, to the day, since that first Valentine rose. With each year, another rose had been added to the bouquet. The roses always arrived punctually at 3:00 p.m. Sandra still had no idea who was sending them. There was never a card. It was never the same delivery person.

Hilda had been retired for five years now and Sandra had taken over her position. Hilda still pestered her about finding someone to share her life with. "Whoever is sending these roses to you every year must really love you," she had said on their last dinner date. "I think you should have made more of an effort to find out who it was!" Hilda's jaw had a firm set to it.

"Well, if they loved me so much they would have shown their face," Sandra had retorted. "Only a coward hides behind roses."

"Maybe he's shy."

"Maybe it's you sending them," Sandra smirked. "Give it up, woman; is it you?" They had laughed. Having been friends for over 30 years, they could say anything to each other.

Sandra glanced at her watch—2:55 p.m. She really should be leaving for work, but the anticipation that had begun to grip her as the years passed held her back. As the cuckoo clock struck 3:00, the doorbell rang. Sandra opened the door and was greeted by a young man with a bouquet of white roses.

"Are you Sandra Mackenzie?"

"Yes."

"I have a dozen and a half roses for you; could you sign here please."

"This is a first," Sandra muttered.

"What's a first?"

"Having to sign."

"That is our new policy."

"Who do you work for?" Sandra asked the question she should have asked years ago.

"Dreamer's Rosery."

"Never heard of it."

"We're not local."

"I see; do you keep a record of purchases?"

"Only those with accounts, or who pay by credit card."

"Any idea who sent these to me?"

"You'll have to call my boss; she might know."

Sandra thanked him with a five dollar tip and closed the door. Her hands trembled as she unwrapped the roses and placed them in the waiting vase. They were beautiful, as usual. Sandra had no idea why she felt so unsettled. She gathered up the paper and stuffed it into the garbage can. She didn't notice the note that dropped to the floor.

James waited in the hospital coffee shop. He looked at his watch—12:45. Maybe she was working late. He knew that happened sometimes. He ordered another coffee and returned to the corner where he had a perfect view of the entrance. He heard the clicking of approaching footsteps and looked up anxiously. It was not her. James rechecked his watch—1:00. He stood and headed for the exit—maybe next year. It had taken all his courage to finally write the note. She had not shown up; therefore, in his mind, it was not meant to be.

Sandra plopped down in a kitchen chair and stared at the white roses. It had been a long shift, and she was tired. "May as well head off to bed; tomorrow is another day." As she stood, she noticed a piece of paper on the floor. "What's this?"

Meet me in the coffee shop on the first level at 12:30 when your shift is finished.

She glanced at her watch—12:45. Finally, her secret admirer had decided to reveal his identity, and she had probably missed him. Sandra grabbed her keys and headed out the door. Hopefully, the mystery of who was sending the white roses would be solved tonight. She entered the hospital through the backdoor employee entrance because it was close to the coffee shop. As she ran in, she didn't notice James getting into the elevator.

"Hi, Millie, was there anyone in here just hanging around? Around 12:30?" she added.

"You working late tonight, Sandra?" Millie inquired.

"Someone sent me a note to meet them here at 12:30; did you notice anyone hanging around?" Sandra repeated.

"Well, James was here, but he just left."

"James?" Sandra knew two James who worked at the hospital. One was a doctor; the other a volunteer. Both had been around for as long as she could remember.

"James Adams." Millie smiled. "You just missed him. He is one heck of a nice guy. Hasn't missed a day here at the hospital since he recovered from his accident. About 30 years ago, wasn't it? My, how time flies! Too bad it left him with all those scars, though; I think he was a good-looking young man … I can tell by the bone structure..." Millie was rambling.

Sandra was out the door. She remembered clearly the day that James had been brought into the hospital. He had been a mess.

She had just graduated and had been working her first shift as a nurse. She remembered how drawn she had been to the young man; how devastated she had been to learn that he had been struck by a drunk driver while on his way home from work. And not just once! As he had tried to get up, the driver had panicked and hit the gas instead of the brakes. He kept hitting James. The final assault had thrown James through a storefront window, showering him with glass.

She had sat with him all through the first night, and over the next two weeks when she was on shift. Even though he was in and out of consciousness, she had read to him. Sometimes she would even hum songs for him, noticing how it soothed him. Sandra remembered being sad when he was finally moved off her floor. She had visited him often when he was in rehab, continuing to read and sing for him. As he improved, he would sometimes hum along with her.

The accident had left James with several permanent facial scars. He walked with a severe limp and suffered significant chronic pain, but he had not used that as a reason to sit around and do nothing. After James was released from the hospital, he had returned and filled out a volunteer form. Life had gone on—she had gotten busy with her career.

Sandra was in the parking lot. She looked around and noticed someone standing at the bus stop. "James!" she called out and waved her hand.

James turned around. The bus was just pulling up.

"James, wait!" Sandra was running now.

James hesitated at the bus door and then, losing his courage, he began to climb up the steps.

Sandra grabbed his arm. "James," she paused; "I believe you were going to buy me a coffee. Sorry, I'm late." She smiled.

"Are you getting on or not, buddy?" the bus driver asked impatiently.

James looked into Sandra's eyes. "No, sir; I'll not be needing a ride tonight," he answered as he reached inside his coat and pulled out a single, white rose.

Fresh Bread

Dedicated to my friend, Zig Misiak

Zig dropped the newspaper. It lay there, on his lap, absorbing the tears that rolled down his cheeks. There are some memories in life that just don't go away—like the smell of fresh-baked bread...

Zig was the oldest of six children. His parents were poorer than dirt, especially in the winter months when his mother was unable to pick up extra cash by working the farmers' fields. That also meant there were no additional fruits or vegetables in the larder. Even though many of what his mother brought home were bruised or cut, they still tasted delightful.

In the winter, the cupboards were almost bare, and there were many times Zig went to school hungry. The food was divided evenly between the six children, and even though Zig was bigger than the rest and in his mind should have had a more substantial portion to fill his stomach, that never happened. In fact, there were days when he was served less—because the babes needed it, his mother would say—and sometimes he would even get nothing.

One day, as Zig was trudging his way through the deep snow to school, he decided to take a different route. In fact, he was thinking not to go to school at all. It was embarrassing when his stomach grumbled, and all the kids would point to him and laugh. It had been one of those mornings when the food was sparse because his dad hadn't been paid yet.

Zig turned down Park Street and followed it downhill to the frozen canal. He thought that maybe if he broke a hole in the ice, he could catch a fish—if not in the channel, he'd head to the river and give it a try.

As Zig closed in on the canal, a savoury aroma filtered into his nostrils—fresh-baked bread. His mouth began to salivate, and his stomach began to churn. As he approached a large red-brick building, the scent became stronger. He noticed an elderly man stepping out of the front door. The man stretched, smiled, and looked up at the sky, then turned back into his store. He flipped a sign on the door: Open.

Zig paused. He patted his pockets, dreaming there might be a coin in one of them with which he could buy a piece of bread. Nothing. He had a thought. Sometimes bakers threw day-old bread out in the dumpsters behind their buildings; maybe this morning would be his lucky day. Zig snuck cautiously down the alleyway and peeked around the corner. All was quiet. He ventured closer to the bin, which was piled high with black garbage bags and clear bags filled with buns. Just as he reached the container, the back door opened, and the elderly man stepped out. Zig froze.

"Good morning, boy." The man's voice grated with age.

"M ... m ... morning," Zig stuttered.

The man smiled. "Don't be scared, boy." He paused, noting the hunger in the boy's eyes and beneath his clothes. "Would you like a bun?" he asked.

Zig's eyes opened wide. "I ... I ... I have no money, sir," he mumbled.

The man smiled again. "No need. My baker over-baked last night; I have some extras in the store." He opened the back door and motioned for Zig to follow him inside. "What's your name, boy?" he asked as he closed the door.

"Zig."

The elderly man put his hand on Zig's shoulder. "Zig. That's a good strong name. Is it short for anything?"

"No." Zig was getting a tad nervous. He knew he should be in school, and he began to wonder at the old man's kindness. Zig was old enough to be acquainted with some of the less pleasant things that went on in the world.

"I am Mr. Bendito," the man stated, "but my friends call me Antony." Mr. Bendito noticed the apprehensive look on Zig's face. He chuckled. "I won't hurt you, Zig ... and you can call me Antony."

The smell of the fresh bread, once again, filled Zig's nostrils. His stomach rumbled. Mr. Bendito reached into a bin and pulled out a large bun, still steaming. He handed it to Zig.

Forgetting his manners, Zig grabbed the bun and bit into it hungrily. The dough melted in his mouth as his saliva went to work.

Mr. Bendito just stood there, smiling. He waited until Zig finished the bun before he spoke again. "Shouldn't you be on your way to school now?"

Zig hung his head and shuffled his feet.

"Well?" Mr. Bendito insisted. He reached into the bin and pulled out another bun. He put it in a paper bag and handed it to Zig. "Your lunch."

Zig reached out nervously and accepted the bag. Mr. Bendito walked to the front door and opened it. "Have a good day, Zig." He paused. "You know, I could use a lad like you to clean up around here; do you think you could come by after school each day and sweep up for me? I close the shop at three-thirty, so the timing will work out perfectly." He paused again. "Ask your parents tonight and let me know in the morning. If they say yes, you can start tomorrow." The door closed.

Zig made his way back down to the street and headed off in the direction of his school. He knew he'd be late, and he would probably get the strap, but it was worth it. The bun was still warm in his tummy, and the one tucked in his coat pocket promised his stomach wouldn't grumble at lunchtime and no one would laugh at him.

Yes, some memories stick with you forever. Zig poured himself a coffee and bit into his early morning crescent. He had worked for Mr. Bendito—Antony—for five years, and then his father had taken a job in another city. Zig had gone off to high school, and then college. He'd kept in touch for a year or so, but then his letters began to be returned, and life had gone on. Time buried the memory of Mr. Bendito—until this morning. Until the notice in the paper.

Zig stood and headed for the door. The smell of fresh-baked bread filled his nostrils as he headed out to attend his old friend's funeral.

Made in the USA
Las Vegas, NV
02 November 2020